Impasse

Impasse

SYLVIE FOX

This edition published by
Penner Publishing
Post Office Box 57914
Los Angeles, California 91413
www.pennerpublishing.com

Copyright © 2013 by Sylvie Fox

ISBN 978-1-944179-35-9

This is a work of fiction. Names, characters, corporations, institutions, organizations, events, or locales in this novel are either the product of the author's imagination or, if real, used fictitiously. The resemblance of any character to actual persons (living or dead) is entirely coincidental.

The author acknowledges the trademarked status and trademark owners of various products referenced in this work of fiction, which have been used without permission. The publication/use of these trademarks is not authorized, associated with, or sponsored by the trademark owners.
Impasse/Sylvie Fox – 2d Edition

Interior designed and formatted by Tianne Samson with emtippettsbookdesigns.com

for Adam

Also by
Sylvie Fox

Romantic Women's Fiction
Unlikely
Impasse
Shaken
Stirred
The Good Enough Husband
Don't Judge Me
The Secret Widow

Legal Thrillers
Qualified Immunity
Under Color of Law
In Plain Sight

One

Holly Prentice wished that a flashing neon sign had put her on alert before her sex life went on hiatus. Maybe she would have paid more attention, perhaps coaxing one more orgasm from her ex. Instead, life without sex had crept up on her silently, stealthily. Two years, one month, and three days had come and gone without any physical satisfaction that she didn't have to initiate and fulfill on her own. Not that she was counting.

Pulling her gaze back to the antique mirror as she sat at her well-worn mahogany vanity, Holly tugged a wide-tooth comb through her wet corkscrew curls and tried to focus her thoughts on the evening ahead. Thirty-two was too damn old to be Sally Field cute. Giving up on hair taming, Holly pulled the dark strands into a loose ponytail and scrutinized herself. Despite her frizzy hair, or maybe because of it, she had to admit she looked younger than her age. Her peaches and cream complexion was smooth and unlined—her face unblemished. Her features were well proportioned. Though she had always found her generous mouth to be a little too wide and her nose more cute than aristocratic.

Applying mascara to the lashes surrounding amber eyes the color of rich honey, she supposed that she was attractive enough. She wouldn't let her smallish breasts or a bit of junk in the trunk keep her at home. She was too old to be insecure over the little things.

Glancing at the brass wind-up clock on her nightstand, she hurried her preparation. It was already seven thirty. Her friend Sophie would be there any minute. She knew her best friend was right. It was time to get out among the living.

More than a year had passed since Holly and her girlfriends made a champagne toast to her new life on the day her divorce became final. She fell out of love with Drew at least two years before she got up the courage to imagine her life without him. He was married to his career as a television executive. She had been eager to settle down, have a baby. Marriage hadn't suited him, and when she told him she wanted more out of life than dinner by the glow of the television—or breakfast with the latest overnight ratings—he had asked for a divorce.

Surprisingly, she was not unhappy by the sudden turn of events. In a way, it had seemed inevitable. The end of their four-year marriage was anti-climactic. She and Drew had amicably divvied up their belongings and gone their separate ways.

They had sold the modern glass and steel showplace they'd called a home for a tidy profit, riding the crest of the last real estate wave in southern California. Holly had socked away her share of the equity for a rainy day. For now, she was happily settled in the top floor apartment of a turn-of-the-century duplex, contemplating her next move. Her next home would be permanent.

Holly heard a soft rapping on the front door and reached down to zip up the soft, brown calfskin boots she'd slipped into before rushing to the living room entrance.

"Girl!" Sophie cried, by way of greeting, and burst into the room. "Are you ready to party?"

Sophie Reid had been Holly's best friend since the day they'd met on the set of one of Drew's nighttime dramas. Looking at the two of them, a stranger would not expect they had much in common. But Holly kept Sophie down to earth, and Sophie added a spirit of adventure to Holly's life.

At a time like this, Sophie was the kind of gal pal Holly needed. She was cute, friendly, and best of all, outgoing. Plus, Sophie had single-handedly taken on the onerous task of getting Holly out among the living, though Holly put on the brakes when it came to blind dating. Like a lot of her peers, she'd put up a picture and profile on popular dating web sites, but she couldn't see dating any of the guys who responded. Half seemed to have no gainful employment, and the other half did not seem interested in her personality. They just sent nude pictures of themselves looking for a one-night hook up. Not a turn-on by any stretch of the imagination.

"Is this okay?" Holly asked pointing to herself and her last minute clothing choice. Donned in snug jeans she had just pulled from the dryer, she had decided on a sheer cashmere sweater over a modest lace camisole. She was hoping she had achieved the casually elegant but still sexy look that dominated nightlife in Los Angeles.

"It's perfect," Sophie said appreciatively. "Though I think you're not wearing a bra." She raised her eyebrows.

Holly laughed, pointing at her breasts, which barely filled an A cup. "Who am I kidding? I only wear a bra to work these days, and that's just for nipple coverage."

Similarly endowed, Sophie laughed and dipped her head knowingly. "No need to dim the headlights tonight," she said laughing. More seriously, she added, "Girl, you're looking really good these days. All that yoga agrees with you."

Not one to sweat it out at the overcrowded gyms that dominated L.A., Holly spent her evenings and weekends on her mat, stretching her muscles and soothing her soul. The result had been a leaner body and a stronger mind. The intense focus on the mind-body exercise had helped her cope with the emotional ups and downs from her divorce. She had tried running on the treadmill at the local gym, but she felt like a hamster on a wheel, in a too-loud disco. Plus, she did not like the insincere come-ons from the unemployed actors who never seemed to stop working out.

Holly grabbed her small, Nova Check Burberry purse—her one nod to luxury in name brand obsessed L.A.—and locked her apartment, following Sophie through the bougainvillea-scented courtyard to her car.

When Holly had gotten the online invite to tonight's cocktail party, she had been set to click the "my glass is empty" button to decline when Sophie wrestled the mouse from her hand.

"Why aren't you going to this party? It sounds like fun."

Before she answered aloud, a million reasons went through

her mind. The housewarming party was being given by a mutual acquaintance of her ex. She would have to navigate the dark, windy roads through the Santa Monica Mountains while studying her Thomas Guide, a driving hazard. Those seemed two excellent reasons to avoid anyone who knew her as Mrs. Drew Burke. Mostly, it would mean socializing with folks from her former married life, and she did not know if she was ready to do that.

"I'm just not ready," was the excuse that came to her lips.

"That's bull. You can't avoid Drew forever," Sophie had said. "They were your friends, too."

Before Holly could protest, Sophie had clicked "I'll drink to that," added herself as a guest, and sent the electronic response. "I'll be here Saturday night to pick you up. No way are you weaseling out of this one."

In the car's dark interior, Holly pulled at her curls nervously as they made their way to the party. She navigated while Sophie drove her sunflower yellow Volkswagen Beetle convertible. Once they wove their way north above Sunset, the city lights gave way to darkness. Following the sharp curves of Benedict Canyon, they made a turn onto Portola Drive, and parked behind a row of cars on the soft shoulder of the road.

The housewarming, or more accurately, a restoration celebration, was at Asha and Hayes' renovated house. Her old friends had purchased one of the former hunting lodges that dotted the hills and canyons of Los Angeles. Holly could appreciate the beautifully subtle lighting and landscaping of the older homes above Beverly Hills.

A number of these wood cabins were built when Los Angeles

was a summer vacation destination of the East Coast rich. None of them were originally suited for year round occupancy, but as Los Angeles quietly moved from one hundred thousand to four million souls in a century, every home became a year-round home.

When she and Drew married, she wanted to purchase a house much like this one or restore one of the beautiful old Craftsman homes near the newly vibrant downtown area. Drew wanted something brand new. He would only consider a showplace of a home to wow his friends and colleagues.

They had ended up in a boxy modern structure with floor-to-ceiling glass windows in the pricey 90210 zip code. Her ex had no sooner hired a Swedish designer than her cherished family heirlooms and comfortable furniture were relegated to permanent storage in exchange for minimalist couches and spindly chairs. She'd never felt comfortable there, so selling their home had been relatively painless. It was if she had never moved in.

"Your friends have a nice looking place," Sophie said, her voice shaded with admiration.

When they walked through the open door at the top of the steep wooden stairs, Holly immediately felt old. The "thumpa, thumpa" bass beat of the music and clinking glasses made her feel like the chaperone at a college frat party. Fortunately, Asha was near the door, eliminating the need to seek out the hostess among the sea of people.

"Asha, it looks like a new house." Holly had to raise her voice to be heard over the music. She thrust her warehouse store bottle at the leggy hostess, hoping no one would read the label and realize she knew nothing about Spanish wine, a request of the hosts.

"I'm so glad you could stop by," Asha said breathily. Asha said everything breathily. She was a beautiful, tall, olive-skinned brunette, with glossy hair falling to her waist, and the faintest hint of a lilting foreign accent. "Please show yourself around. It's small, but we like it. Tonight we have pomegranate martinis. Hayes is tending bar," she finished, winking.

Holly felt Sophie fidgeting behind her.

"Asha, I'm sure you remember Sophie."

"Yes, lovely to see you again," she said, air kissing Sophie's cheeks before drifting off to mingle with other newly arriving guests.

There seemed to be more than fifty people crammed into the small space. Sophie led the way to the farmhouse table where Hayes was shaking and pouring jewel red martinis.

Hayes came from around the table and gave Holly a warm hug.

"It's so good to see you. How's Drew?" he asked automatically before pausing, when Holly just shrugged.

"I really stuck my foot in it, didn't I?" Hayes said shamefacedly, resuming his pouring duties as guests snapped up the fruity drinks. "Well, he was a fool to lose you. Please, have a drink and mingle." He added bright green lime wedges to drinks he had just mixed and handed one each to her and Sophie.

Even though they did not move in the same social circles—it seemed that Sophie knew everyone in town—a boisterous group of below-the-line crew swept her friend into their circle, leaving Holly alone.

Impasse

Sipping her martini, Holly decided to give herself a tour of the small home. Built into the hillside, all the rooms were on the second and third floors. Holly loved the couple's attention to detail in the remodeling effort. The freshly decorated bedrooms had gleaming oak floors, polished golden, and antique brass beds.

Not ready to join the crowd downstairs, she tucked herself quietly into a cushioned Adirondack chair on the deck off the master bedroom. She could feel the vibration of the music and the dancing of the people on the landing just below. Holly blotted them out as she finished her martini and looked up at the few stars she could see twinkling in the night sky.

Despite the crowd below, Holly thought she had picked an isolated spot. She was startled when Sophie came out onto the deck carrying fresh drinks.

"I knew you'd be holed up somewhere. You should come on down. Everybody's having a great time."

Holly pushed her curls back from her face and shook her head. "I'll mingle in a bit. I'm not ready to have everyone ask me about Drew and his latest project."

When Sophie gave her a hard look, Holly tilted her head, relenting. "I promise. I'll come down." Sophie did not push, but gave her a squeeze on the shoulder before rejoining the party. Holly drew up her legs and listened to the distant howling of dogs, coyotes, or some kind of feral animals.

She sighed audibly. It was all so hard. She had been part of Holly and Drew—or "The Burkes"—for so long, it was difficult to think of herself as a single person. God knows, she was lonely at night but could not imagine answering any of those creepy

Internet dating ads or going through a series of bad blind dates in search of Mr. Right.

When she heard footsteps coming toward the deck this time, she assumed it was Sophie coming back to cajole her into a better mood, but she was surprised instead to see the profile of a man, his face obscured by the darkness.

From what she could see, he was hot with a capital H. Why couldn't someone like this tall drink of water spill into her life? The casual knit shirt he wore, pulled across his broad chest, and lay across a washboard flat stomach. Was that a sexy bomber jacket, too? She loved long, thick, dark hair, and his fell over his forehead in such a way that her hands itched to brush it back. His distressed jeans hugged him in all the right places. He had bad boy written all over him. She'd always been a good girl with bad boy fantasies. Maybe it was time to end her celibate period and indulge in a few.

Right now.

Tonight.

"Holly, is that you?"

Wait, she knew that voice.

"Nick?" she asked uncertainly.

When he stepped fully onto the deck, Holly's breath stuck in her throat, then hissed out slowly.

Thank goodness.

It was just Nick.

She could put off a close encounter with an available member of the opposite sex for another day.

Nick Andreis had worked with her husband before Drew had made the jump from cable television to network, and Nick had moved from TV to documentaries. But he had been more than just a colleague of her husband's. He had been one of their good friends. She didn't realize until that moment how much she missed his company and that of their other mutual friends. Sophie had been right about her coming to this party.

She'd met Nick about five years before, when he was fresh out of college and her ex was mentoring him at the network. She and Drew had sort of taken Nick under their wing. He'd been that young guy who came over for home cooked meals dozens of times. She'd seen movies with Nick and palled around with him while her ex-husband had been working. None of that history could explain the sudden flutter in her heart. It wasn't as if Nick were some attractive guy she'd just met for the first time at a party. He was just Nick, really. Still, tonight, for reasons Holly couldn't quite put her finger on, Nick took her breath away. Had he been this handsome and virile all these years? Had she been this lonely and shamelessly hard-up before?

Surreptitiously, she gave him a good once over. Life was obviously agreeing with him. He was all planes and angles, hard muscles, and beautiful hair. She'd always treated him like a little brother, but the feelings he inspired this evening were anything but fraternal.

Holly put her empty martini glass on the table and stood up to hug him. When he enveloped her in his strong arms, she hoped he didn't notice her quick intake of breath or feel the acceleration of her pulse.

"It's been too long since I've seen you," she said, her voice muffled by his broad chest. He felt so warm and smelled wonderful—like soap and man. The embrace, which should have been customarily brief, went on a beat too long, her thoughts straying to warm nights and hot sheets.

Pulling away, she shook her head trying to dispel her wayward thoughts. Suddenly aware of a nervousness she hadn't felt in years around a man, she shoved her jittery hands in her back pockets. The loneliness of her self-imposed celibacy must be getting to her.

"What are you doing up here all by yourself?" he asked.

"Just enjoying the night," she said. "It's weird how age affects you. Suddenly you wake up one day, you're past thirty, and it feels like music at parties is too loud and drinks are too strong." They were each quiet for a few moments, the tension between them suddenly as thick as pea soup.

"Holly, it's great to see you," Nick said breaking the silence. "You never answered any of my emails."

When had his voice gotten so deep? His rich baritone resonated within her, and she felt a responsive quiver far down in her stomach. She'd clearly missed Nick's transformation from college graduate to full-fledged man.

"I..."

"No need to explain," he said, seating himself in the middle of the rattan couch, drawing her cold hands from her pockets, and pulling her down next to him. "It's just good to see you. You look great. I mean you look really good," he said earnestly.

Something about the way he complimented her seemed more than superficial, but she didn't probe it and scooted a few inches from him on the couch so she could look directly into his vivid green eyes.

"How's your—"

Impasse

"What are you—"

Their words crashed into each other, and they both laughed, dispelling some of the awkwardness. They'd been friends for years; she didn't know why she was suddenly feeling uncomfortable around Nick.

"You first," she said, pulling her hand back and rubbing both of them together for warmth.

He clasped her hands in his large ones again, massaging them briskly this time. "You're cold. Here, take my jacket."

Before she could protest, he stood and removed the sexy-as-hell brown bomber jacket from his broad shoulders and wrapped it around her. He then rubbed her arms for good measure. His touch alone warmed her. Correction: his touch made her hot. She loved being wrapped in his jacket, even though she didn't need it to keep her warm. As long as he was near, her body generated enough body heat to ward off the desert night chill. The jacket smelled of leather, saddle soap, and Nick. She couldn't remember being this turned on just sitting next to, and not even touching, a man.

Nick didn't say anything. He just looked at her with something akin to longing in his eyes. Feeling the need to fill the silence, to look away from his smoky green eyes, the golden flecks simmering with something like desire, Holly started asking questions, talking about anything to dispel the awkwardness that had returned as soon as he touched her.

"So, how is your house? I haven't really seen it since you made the offer on it."

Nick smiled, a tiny dimple appearing on his chin. She'd always enjoyed talking to him about this favorite interest they shared. Holly loved making a warm and cozy living space, and she was amazed that he'd taken on the task of remodeling his own home, even with his busy work schedule as a documentary filmmaker.

"Since you were last there, I've finished the kitchen but still have the bathrooms and laundry to do. Not to mention a whole lot of painting." Nick paused as if he were making up his mind about something. "Hey, why don't you come see it?"

"Now?" Holly thought quickly. He couldn't be more than a mile away. It would be better than spending more time at this party. Even from up here, the loud music was getting to her. Nevertheless, she hesitated.

She was feeling vulnerable and didn't know if tonight was a good time to be alone with a virile, single, very sexy man—no matter how safe and innocent their meeting seemed. She didn't want her aging libido to overwhelm her and cause her to do something embarrassing. Something was lurking between them, but she wanted to keep it carefully submerged where she could exercise some control over her feelings and behavior.

"C'mon. Why not? We can walk over," he said cajoling. "Are you here with Sophie?"

"Of course I'm here with Sophie." Holly laughed. "You know how she thrives on these kinds of parties. I'm sure you saw her cranberry colored, spiked hair in the crowd. I think she dyed her hair to match the martinis."

Nick laughed, his baritone as smooth as single malt scotch, and grabbed her hand to pull her up. The jolt of touching his large, roughened hand again, shook her to the core. Surely, she couldn't be attracted to Nick. He was…just Nick.

Impasse

Holly was sure he was just being his usual gallant self, and that there was nothing more to his touch than good old-fashioned chivalry. Yet there she was getting all hot and bothered in his mere presence. She was glad his jacket hid her pebbled nipples, and obscured the moment when she squeezed her thighs together to stem the tide of longing she felt. She desperately hoped he didn't notice her body's response to his touch. Holly stood and tried to pull away feeling as transparent as plastic wrap.

But Nick held her hand firmly. "C'mon. We'll tell Sophie we're out of here. I'm sure she'll get home just fine without you."

They found her friend downstairs sharing the punch line of an obviously bawdy joke. Holly snatched her hand from Nick's, but not before Sophie raised her pierced eyebrow speculatively. Sophie pulled herself away from the group and came over to where they were standing.

"Hey, Sophie, I'm going to see what Nick's done with the house." Holly ran her now free hands through her wild curls, pulling out the hair band tangled in the mess. Anything to keep her fingers occupied and away from Nick's. "He's been renovating it himself. Well, he and his dad, actually. Do you mind? Can you say my goodbyes to Asha and Hayes?" Holly mentally chastised herself. When did she become so chatty? She hoped neither Nick nor Sophie noticed the slight quaver in her voice or how nervous she was.

"Holly, it's all good," Sophie said, waving her away. "Go with Nick. I'm sure he'll take care of you. Don't worry about me. Just have fun."

Luckily, Holly missed the wink Sophie gave him as they turned to leave the party, or the woman next to him might have changed her mind. Nick took a deep breath and tried to calm the beating of his heart. He had almost embarrassed himself. Seeing her nipples bead under her thin sweater, he couldn't stop thinking about using his thumb to brush their tips, his tongue to make her harder, or putting his mouth on her. Thank God she'd put his jacket on. The snap of cold night air seeping through his clothes cooled his arousal. He was saved from having to lope through the hills bent over like the hunchback of Notre Dame.

He wasn't too proud to admit to himself that he'd had quite a few fantasies about getting Holly alone during the last year of on-and-off contact with her. He'd tried dating other women and hanging out with the guys to get his mind off of her. Sometimes it even worked for a while.

But in the quiet of night, or when he was meticulously working on some aspect of the house, his thoughts would always stray back to her. Holly was inextricably woven into the rich tapestry that was his fantasy life. It was a little overwhelming to realize that finally, he was about to have her all to himself—on his turf—no distractions.

When he'd first met Holly all those years before, he'd thought of her as no more than his mentor's wife. But after years of spending time with her and Drew, he'd come to realize that Drew didn't love her—not the way she needed to be loved. Drew constantly worked to give Holly what he thought she wanted. A big house, expensive clothes, and ostentatious jewelry. From spending time with Holly, it was obvious to anyone who paid attention that she had simple but excellent taste, and she wasn't in a relationship for what her husband could give her, unlike a lot of materialistic women in L.A. who would have happily traded places with her.

Nick figured Drew never came to that realization. Their divorce had relieved him of his guilt. By then, he'd fully understood that his interest in Holly was more than platonic. Childishly, he had hoped that Holly would lean on him after the divorce. Part of his fantasies sometimes involved him helping her work through her grief as she realized that he was the man for her. But when she'd turned inward instead, he'd realized he might have been watching too many of those sappy romantic comedies on late night satellite television.

As time passed and their contact became more sporadic, Nick didn't quite know how to approach her and reestablish their relationship. When she didn't respond to the few casual emails he'd sent at first, he'd tried to move on. But he couldn't shake her from his thoughts.

Clicking through his email tonight, he had seen her name on the electronic party invitation's "I'll drink to that" list. Motivated, he'd shaved for the second time that day, put on his most casual-but-makes-me-look-good shirt, and walked over to the party.

At the bottom of Asha and Hayes' front stairs, she turned around, and her unruly curls blew across her face. Absently, she tucked her hair behind her ears. "I'm lost without my Thomas Guide. Which way is it to your place?"

It was true that almost nobody walked in L.A., but he was glad for the time outside. The brisk canyon air cooled his heated body. He tried desperately to think about anything other than Holly, or her body, or what he'd like to do with her body. Looking down, it was obvious that neither the cold air, nor trying to think of other things hadn't worked because he wasn't in a much better state now. He still felt the jeans rubbing uncomfortably against his erection, which had come back with full force.

Walking behind her wasn't helping the matter, either, except that fortunately for him, she couldn't see the evidence of his desire. The snug jeans she wore hugged her full bottom and tapered to her tiny waist, setting his teeth on edge. Coupled with her wrapped in the jacket he'd worn just minutes ago, he felt an almost primal link to her.

Deliberately, he grabbed her hand again. Even that small palm-to-palm contact gave him a nervous stomach but solidified what he hoped was a growing connection. "Just follow me. It's down the hill a bit."

He held fast to her hand, keeping her close and away from the occasional but swiftly moving cars. None of these old rural streets had sidewalks, and he needed to keep her safe as they walked along Benedict Canyon's soft berm. They turned onto his street, Easton Drive, and she pulled away from him, smoothing back her flyaway hair.

Nick was almost sure she was as nervous as he because she had a little attraction for him as well. He was secretly thrilled that she had any reaction at all. Maybe he wasn't out in left field with his feelings for this woman. If there was the smallest chance she would return his feelings, he could work with that. A chance was all he needed—he'd handle everything else from there.

His wood-sided house finally came into view; it had been built in the eighties but hadn't been well maintained over the last two decades. For that reason, he'd gotten a steep discount on the price, but in lieu of a big mortgage payment, he'd had to put in months of sweat equity to make the place livable. The weather-beaten, blue-gray, wood-shingled home was three stories, with two bedrooms, two baths, and a loft overlooking the master bedroom.

"Nick, have you been landscaping?" she asked, and he was grateful for any conversation topic to ease the tension mounting between them.

"Yeah, sort of, but I don't think you'll be able to see it in the dark. C'mon on in and let me show you what my dad and I have done."

Like Asha and Hayes' house, they had to ascend narrow, dimly lit stairs to get to the main rooms on the second floor. He flicked on the lights and felt a small swelling of pride in his work when she gasped.

"Wow," she said.

The walls that had once been deeply marred were now a smooth, primed canvas ready for a splash of color. The delicately coved ceiling had been scraped clean of its former pocked cottage-cheese coating. But Holly seemed most delighted with his completed kitchen. He'd chosen to stain the original oak cabinets with a honey hue, and added all new stainless steel appliances tucked neatly into the warm-colored cabinets. Nick watched as she stroked the brown, black, and red-flecked granite, imagining her cooking in his kitchen.

When she finally looked up at him with admiration shining in her eyes, he suppressed an urge to gather her in his arms and swing her around with a shout of triumph.

"This is great. I mean, spectacular. When I first saw the

place, I never imagined it like this. Can I see upstairs?" she asked eagerly.

"It's really dark. Let me go first," he said. "I haven't fixed all the lights."

Nick grabbed Holly's hand again, thrilled at their contact, and led her up the narrow, winding stairs. When she stumbled a little at the top, he took the opportunity to embrace her loosely.

"I'm so sorry," she stammered. "I'm such a klutz."

The feel of her gentle curves under his heavy leather jacket were almost his undoing. He had to make this tour quick and get back downstairs on solid ground. He went hard, again, at the thought of her in his bedroom, in his bed. Nick reluctantly let her go. He didn't want to scare her or embarrass himself with his inability to control his reaction. Like a good host, he turned on a hallway light and continued the tour, careful to angle his body away from her view.

He showed Holly the outdated black, pink, and green tiled bathrooms, talking about the changes he would like to make, using natural stone and warm colors. After a short walk down the short hall, Nick turned on the only bedroom lamp, casting his darkened room in a soft yellow glow. The only other room in the house near completion, it was dominated by a king-size sleigh bed and stately mahogany wardrobe.

Nick led her to the arched floor-to-ceiling windows that faced the street. He eased his jacket from her shoulders and tossed it carelessly on the bed, fully appreciating the curves Holly's lacy sweater revealed. With the light shining behind her, her sheer clothing left little to the imagination. And that was a good thing. He was done imagining. He was ready for the real deal.

Impasse

"You don't have any curtains," she said matter-of-factly.

"Don't worry, no one can see in," he reassured her. He walked over and turned out the lights. When she gasped in surprise, he said, "Wait. You have to see this." Once their eyes adjusted, he gestured to the view of the canyon. The sky was a blanket of stars; the ground a sea of lights from the homes that dotted the hills. He knew, from many nights staring at this view that the effect was enchanting.

"It's beautiful. This is so amazing, everything that you've done."

"I love it here. It's like sleeping under the stars."

Nick came over to stand behind Holly at the window, resisting the urge to gather her in his arms and rest his chin on her wild mane. Instead, he placed a hand somewhat awkwardly on her shoulder. His voice was serious when he spoke. "I missed spending time with you."

The room was too dark, Nick too close. Flustered, Holly struggled to say something, anything to get her out of the bedroom. "Um, it's great seeing you, too. Do you mind if I use your bathroom?" Holly excused herself before she did anything she might regret later. She fled to the closest bathroom, closed the door, turned around, and sagged against the heavy wood. She listened to Nick's footsteps fading as he headed back down the stairs.

Was he coming on to her? This was starting to feel less like a couple of platonic friends getting together and more like a first or even second date. She fumbled for the bathroom light switch and looked in the mirror. Maybe she was imagining things. She looked the same—a little flushed, maybe. Did he see something different in her? In the years they had known each other, she couldn't remember ever thinking about him in that way—man to woman.

Holly was certainly attracted to him now. Just touching his hand made the butterflies, which seemed to have taken up permanent residence in her stomach, take flight. She couldn't ignore what even a blind woman could see—that he was hotter than the thirty-two candles on her last birthday cake. They'd always gotten along well and had a lot of fun together, but even as lonely as she was, she didn't seriously think she could have a relationship with someone six years her junior. Plus, he didn't even have a couch.

She splashed her face with cool water, hoping to hide the telltale signs of her arousal. Staring at her reflection, she listed the reasons she couldn't pursue even a one-night hook-up with Nick. Like any other single woman who'd been burned, she'd established rules that would govern her future choices.

First, he couldn't be married to a wife or his career. Second, he had to want a family. As corny as it may seem, she wanted children, a dog, maybe even a white picket fence, and she didn't want to start something with a man who didn't share her vision of the future, even if it was just for hot sex. Third, she needed a man who was settled down. In addition, she thought as she patted her cheeks dry with a hand towel, she needed a new rule, just for Nick: He had to have a couch.

Having ground rules in place, Holly felt much more secure as she turned off the taps. Looking around, she expanded her criteria. Her new rule should be to only date men with couches, real furniture, and paint. Definitely paint should be a requirement. Holly counted on her fingers. Was that five or six? She caught a glance at her hand-me-down tank watch. It was ten o'clock. She could probably leave now without seeming rude. Holly knew if she put some distance between them, then she would surely come to her senses.

When Holly got downstairs, she noticed a perceptible shift in the atmosphere of the bare living room. It looked the same as before, dominated by his large, flat screen TV. But newly flickering firelight made the room glow warm. Large pillows she hadn't noticed before were lying on a large rug before the fireplace. It screamed bachelor pad, and the mood was set for seduction. She knew then that she definitely wasn't imagining his attraction to her. Nick had even made them a small picnic—of wine, cheese, and bread—definitely a feast for temptation.

Thank goodness for age and wisdom. "Oh, Nick. You didn't have to do all this… " Holly faltered. Too bad age hadn't improved her ability to talk herself out of awkward situations. She didn't know what else to say. "I'm feeling a little funny," she said motioning to her midsection. It was the best excuse she could come up with on short notice. "Maybe it's time for me to go." It sounded lame even to her own ears. But, if she left now, she could be sure of controlling herself around him.

"Did you eat at all tonight?"

"No, not since lunch."

"Just sit then. Eat a little. You really shouldn't drink red martinis on an empty stomach," he said with a smile.

Stay or go? Holly should go home. Her adult brain was telling her to leave, now. If she stayed, she knew what could happen.

Sex with Nick. It was like she had a little angel on one shoulder and a little devil on the other. Her devil, who looked remarkably like Sophie, wanted her to stay. The angel was mutinously silent. Her neglected libido won out over reason. Damned martinis. It was common knowledge that alcohol was the sworn enemy of common sense.

She joined him on the faux fur rug before the fireplace, sitting as far away as the rug would allow. Holly fiddled with her watch, not meeting Nick's eyes.

"Holly, please relax. We won't do anything you don't want." His words fell like stones in a still pond, the ripples teasing her senses. Did he want her? What did she want? After what seemed like forever, Nick handed her a glass of wine and spoke again. "Please tell me what's been going on with you this past year. I feel like I've missed so much. I need to catch up on your life."

She could do this—have a normal conversation. Holly mustered up her courage and looked into Nick's deep, green eyes. Yes, she felt a genuine fondness for an old friend. There was also that zing of attraction that gave her goose bumps and further tightened her already beaded nipples. She tried to focus on the former feeling when she answered him.

"Nick, I'm really happy for the first time in a long time." When she said it, Holly realized it was true. "I'm finally living a life I've always wanted. I'm in this lovely old grand dame of a Spanish building surrounded by my grandmother's furniture and antiques. I love my neighborhood, and I can walk to a bunch of shops and restaurants. It's pretty cool." Nick didn't break eye contact, or speak, but nodded encouragingly while sipping his own wine.

Impasse

"Work is going well, also. I've changed positions since the last time I talked to you. I feel like I'm doing something a lot more meaningful." Holly described her new role at Equia Children's Entertainment, which was approaching its centennial as the most well-known animation studio in Los Angeles. Located away from the hustle and bustle of the other studios, near the ocean in Venice, its Otto the Otter trademark was almost as recognizable as Mickey Mouse. After her divorce, she switched from marketing and promotion to community outreach.

Promoting the latest animated movie and related merchandise to little kids had lost its luster. Instead, sharing the studio's largesse with the less fortunate citizens of the greater Los Angeles community was truly where her heart was. It was her job to distribute corporate grants to community non-profits and organize employees to volunteer for local charities.

"I guess I'm finally where I want to be in life," she paused, thoughtful. "I'm ready to settle down, get married, have kids— the whole shebang," Holly finished, and realized that Nick was really listening to her, not just nodding to appease her as Drew often had. Feeling more at ease, she took a large sip of the red wine in her glass and ate a wedge of soft, deliciously pungent cheese followed by a chunk of bread.

When she relaxed, she began having more fun than she'd had at that loud party. They talked, ate, and laughed into the early hours of the morning. Nick regaled Holly with all the triumphs and mishaps of his remodeling efforts. Feeling warm—whether from the wine, the fire, or the company, she didn't know—Holly took off her boots and sweater and curled up in a luxuriously soft throw Nick had handed her at some point. Feeling her eyelids droop, then become heavier and heavier, she let sleep overtake her.

Nick gently removed the empty wine glass from her hand, gathered their picnic remains, and carried them to the kitchen. He pulled another plush pillow toward Holly and propped her head on it. He tucked the throw more securely around her shoulder, eased her into the crook of his shoulder, and lay down next to her, watching her doze.

He stroked her bare arms, amazed at the softness of her skin. His breathing quickened as he watched her nipples pucker. When the fire died and the temperature dropped in the room. He slid the throw down to get a better look at her lithe body under the whisper-thin camisole. Damn, he'd forgotten she'd ditched the sweater. There was only the thinnest silky thing between him and her. It was obvious that she wore no bra. He was only a whisper away from her pebble hard nipples. It took all his might to keep his hands away from her skin.

God, she was beautiful. Nick watched the fading firelight flicker on her dewy skin and soft lips, pouty with sleep. He couldn't believe Drew had walked out on someone as wonderful, as giving, as beautiful as Holly. He admired Drew for his work ethic and business savvy, but when it came this woman, Drew had lost his mind.

Unable to resist touching her again, he ran a hand through her silken curls, then brushed her warm cheek with the back of his hand. Nick snatched it back, caught off guard once again by the swift reaction of his groin and the unexpected quiver in body. He couldn't believe how much he wanted her. He'd been thinking about her all of these months, and her presence in his house, where he'd fantasized about making love to her time and again, was killing him slowly. He could think of only one way to relieve the pressure.

"Holly," he whispered gently, stroking her hair, waking her.

"What?" She awakened and eyed him sleepily, her golden cat-like eyes reflecting the dying firelight. "Do you want me to get ready to go?" she asked rustling under the throw.

"No," he stilled her with a large firm hand on her hip. "I need to… " Her sleepy amber-flecked eyes, luminous in the smoldering fire, looked confused and a little unfocused. Nick let out a breath he didn't realize he was holding. Stroking her lip with the calloused pad of his thumb, he continued. "Holly, I desperately need to kiss you right now." Nick caught her hair in his hands and fitted his mouth to hers.

Two

Nick's firm, sensual lips against Holly's soft ones felt like heaven. She should have known it would feel like this between them when each touch had almost sent her through the roof tonight.

Every brush of his lips across hers, each stroke of his tongue created a persistent thrumming down below. Even though she had been warm beneath the throw, Holly shivered when his large hand stroked her side, the pad of his thumb grazing her nipple. Nick broke off the kiss and stared hard at her, longing clear in his eyes.

She started to pull herself out of his arms. "Nick, I don't think this is good idea."

"Don't think," Nick said very slowly and deliberately before taking her lips again. Holly couldn't believe this amazing mouth belonged to Nick. In all the years she had known him, she couldn't have imagined they would fit together this well. It was like she had found the missing piece of a puzzle. Drowning in sensation, she wasn't aware that Nick had eased her silky camisole above her breasts until she felt the chill air caress her bare chest.

Holly moved to pull her tank back down. "Nick, I'm kind of small up top," she said, flustered. She wasn't ready for this, for him to see her breasts lit by the few smoldering embers casting a weak light in the room.

"Holly," Nick said, stopping her hand. "You're so beautiful, so perfect, and just right for me." Holly relaxed a little, until Nick's head swooped down and captured a puckered, dusky pink nipple between his lips, alternately sucking, then licking until she was gasping for breath.

It had been so long since Holly had felt this good, this cherished, this wanted.

"I've waited years for this," Nick whispered. He blew on her overheated flesh. "Let me pleasure you."

Intellectually, Holly knew being with Nick was wrong, but it felt so right. She was looking for Mr. Right—someone in it for the long haul—marriage, a house, and babies. Nick was a young guy looking for Ms. Right Now. Still, rational thoughts fled when he touched her again.

She could feel the aching loneliness of the last two long years ebbing away. For tonight, she wanted more than anything to take the pleasure he was giving—to be his Right Now. When he captured her lips this time, she threw caution to the wind and returned his kiss with conviction.

What felt like seconds, minutes, or hours later—she couldn't tell—he reluctantly pulled his mouth from hers, breathing heavily. Disentangling their arms, he settled her gently on a plush pillow and trailed his hands through her hair, a finger across her lips. He stroked the insides of her arms, traced her aureoles, then dipped his head to gently nip at the indentation of her navel, his hair grazing her belly.

Holly sucked in her breath in anticipation when Nick unbuttoned her jeans—his wonderfully male smell overwhelming her. She lifted her arm to stroke his hard chest and rippled stomach through his shirt. His body was warmer and harder than it looked. Holly's hips bucked when Nick slid a finger into the waistband of her lacy boy shorts and brushed against her dampened curls. Nick's eyes glowed emerald with his desire.

"Holly, I never imagined you'd be this warm, this responsive," Nick breathed.

He tugged her jeans down and blew softly at the area between the apex of her thighs. Her lacy, black panties followed the path of her jeans, and she thought she was going to melt. All of Holly's modesty flew out the window when his lips fastened on her sex, and his tongue teased her clitoris. He positioned her legs over his shoulders, his tongue darting and flicking. His hands skimmed up her sides to palm her small breasts, his roughened fingertips massaging her erect nipples. The combination of his soft tongue and strong fingers caused her womb to tighten. His dilated pupils made his green eyes looked almost black.

Distantly, she thought she heard her own whimpers and cries of ecstasy. Her hips flexed of their own volition, placing her sex closer to his expert ministrations. She was so close, hanging over the edge of the precipice. When he removed one hand from her breast and inserted a finger inside her, she exploded, the years of celibacy bringing about her quick release.

Impasse

Her cries echoed off the unfinished walls of the house. Nick's hard, hot, denim-covered erection brushed against her leg as he gathered her in his arms. Instinctively, Holly reached down to stroke his length, to bring him the same pleasure and release he had brought her. Nick gently pulled her hand away, lacing his fingers with hers.

"Shhh. It's late," he said, smoothing her hair.

"But—"

"I'm okay. I wanted to make you feel good."

He gathered the throw over both of them, murmuring words of comfort, words of tenderness, until she fell into a deep sleep.

The bare, arched windows gave way to the bright California sunshine around seven the next morning. The fire had burned down, and she was shivery with only a thin silk camisole and blanket covering her body. She stretched languidly, reveling in the feeling of blissful release, until memories from the previous night came flooding back.

Her body snapped back like a rubber band, blood rushing to her face and chest. Fortunately, Nick wasn't in the room to witness her face flame. Holly wasn't displeased by their lovemaking exactly. But it was an especially vulnerable time after the years of celibacy. She was discomfited that she'd taken that journey with her much younger friend. Sex could ruin friendships. Holly fervently hoped that they could go back to the way they used to be.

Holly quickly located her panties and pulled the lacy black scrap on, then shimmied into her jeans. She was leaning on the deep windowsill, zipping her boots when Nick brought her a steaming mug of tea. The sweet scent of Darjeeling wafted by her nostrils even before she sipped.

Handing her the tea, he smiled. "Here, why don't you drink this?"

She couldn't believe he remembered she liked tea in the morning. It was a relic of so many mornings spent with her English grandmother. She'd mentioned it to him only once, years ago.

Finger combing her unruly hair, Holly lifted her lashes to look at Nick. Too uneasy to speak, she sipped her tea, suddenly fascinated by the swirling brew. Before she could gather her thoughts to say anything, Nick's deep voice filled the air.

"Holly." He tipped up her chin until she was looking directly into his eyes. "I don't regret anything that happened between us. I need you to know that."

Setting her mug down on the sill, she worked to gather the courage to talk. She wanted to say so many things: how incredible last night had been. That he was an unbelievable kisser. He had made her feel more cherished that she'd been in a long time. How she would like to spend more time getting to know him, man to woman, even if it wasn't a good idea. But none of that seemed right. Despite all that, the inappropriateness of a relationship with someone this young clamored in her mind.

"Nick, I think you should take me home now," was the only sentence she could muster.

His green eyes were murky and unreadable when he spoke. "Finish your tea. I'll get my keys."

When he jogged upstairs without protest, Holly was slightly disheartened. She knew she was just a one-night stand, of sorts, but was a little disappointed that he was willing to shake her off so quickly. Though she didn't want to probe too deeply at the source of those feelings because it made no sense for her to be upset. She knew they could go no farther than they had the night before, but she wanted him to want more even if she couldn't acquiesce. Shaking her head to dispel her traitorous thoughts, she finished her tea, then knotted her sheer cashmere sweater across her shoulders.

The ride down the hill was mercifully silent. The top was down on his small two-seater, luxury convertible, but she still felt confined in the small cabin of the Mercedes. His every movement reminded her of the pleasures of the night before. From his flexed forearms, tanned and lightly dusted with fine hairs, turning the leather-covered steering wheel, to his strong, blunt-tipped fingers manipulating the gearshift. She could almost feel those capable hands caressing her still-heated flesh.

The streets of the city were deserted, and when he pulled up to her small duplex, she had her hand on the door handle before the car came to a full stop. She needed to escape the car and the cliché of the predatory older woman cougar taking advantage of a vulnerable younger man.

His deliberate hand on her forearm stilled her movement.

"Holly?"

She turned toward him, already drowning in the pools of his green eyes.

"I want to see you again," he said.

She flooded with relief that he still wanted her as much as she wanted him. Reality quickly set in, and she shook her head, almost involuntarily. "Nick, you're a great guy, but this cannot happen again."

The hurt she thought she saw in his clear green gaze surprised her. Holly ignored it and spoke quickly. "Nick, don't get me wrong. Last night was unexpected—but nice. It just can't happen again.

"You know that I recently ended a relationship with someone who was out for a good time, living for the here and now." He started to speak, but she plowed on, silencing him. "I'm at a stage in my life where I know what I want. And that's marriage, a child or two, permanency.

"You're young. You have a lot more experimenting to do. I want you to enjoy it. The twenties were some of the best years of my life, and they should be for you as well. A relationship with me would just hold you back. But call me sometime, I'd love to hear how things are going—come to your official housewarming party, maybe just get together."

Holly was proud at having closed this door in her life so maturely, before it had opened too far. She might be wildly attracted to Nick, but she was mature enough now to know that lust wasn't everything. It wasn't forever.

She leaned over to give him a goodbye peck on the cheek. He turned his head toward hers and caught her in a dizziness-inducing kiss, his hands stroking her hair, caressing her soft cheek. Reluctantly, Holly pulled away. She almost ran from his car, through the courtyard, to her apartment. Once she was safely behind the solid wood door of her second floor flat, she could breathe easier. She didn't know what had come over Nick, or her for that matter, but she needed to work him out of her system—the sooner, the better.

Impasse

Holly undressed, leaving a clothes strewn path to the bathroom door. If she just showered, maybe she could forget what had happened. Yet the pulsing hot spray did nothing to erase the memories of Nick's tender worship of her body. Even the touch of her own fingers washing and conditioning her hair sent shockwaves of awareness up and down the nerve endings of her spine.

Done with her mass of curly hair, Holly jumped from the shower and her double crossing showerhead, dried off quickly, and threw on her candy pink velour sweats and hoodie. Slipping into comfortable, thick terry socks, she was determined not to spend her Sunday thinking about Nick's mouth making love to hers, Nick's tongue giving her the most intimate of kisses, or Nick's fingers strumming her body like a well-played Fender guitar.

Holly was in the kitchen deciding between a pint of chocolate marshmallow ice cream goodness or an early yoga class when she heard her instant messaging program trill from her small office in the second bedroom. Closing the freezer, Holly walked to her office and opened her laptop to see who wanted to chat.

It was Sophie, of course.

> **Sophiegrrl**: Are you there? You shouldn't be. Should I try you at Nick's?
> **XmasChick**: Ha ha. Very funny. I'm right here.
> **Sophiegrrl**: Why aren't you with that hunk of man you went home with last night?
> **XmasChick**: I didn't go home with him exactly.
> **Sophiegrrl**: What would you call it then?

XmasChick: Whatever. Anyway, I'm at my house because I'm not a cradle robber.

Sophiegrrl: Nick is sooo hot. Why are you dissing a great guy who obviously wants to get with you? DO NOT message me back. I'm coming over right now to knock some sense into you.

By the time Sophie arrived, Holly had made a large dent in the pint of ice cream. Sophie helped herself to a spoon, and joined Holly on the couch. Both rested their stocking feet on the low coffee table, the ice cream between them.

"So what's the story? Did you sleep with him last night?"

Heat crept into Holly's cheeks. "No," she paused for a moment too long. "Not exactly. Why would you think that?"

"Holly, 'cause you're my girl, I'm going to level with you. Nick has a thing for you. I mean he has it bad. Anybody looking at that man can see he's gone all gaga over you. I may be wildly speculating here, but it's my guess that when you left Drew, he realized how much he wanted to be with you. Last night, I'm sure he came to Asha's party just because you were there. It's not like he was talking to anyone else. How did you think he found you? That was me, helping with the hook-up."

"You were helping Nick?" Holly asked, confused.

"Am I missing something? Why the Häagan Dazs and the long face? The hottest guy this side of the Rocky Mountains goes out of his way to seek you out, and you're drowning yourself in a pint of rocky road ice cream."

"Oh Sophie, don't get me wrong. Nick's a really nice guy. And if I were just out for a fling, I might try him out for a whirl.

But I already made this mistake once with Drew. I want a man who's ready to settle down. Nick's twenty-six. I already married a twenty-six-year-old once. I doubt he knows where his next meal is coming from, much less his next relationship. Sophie, he doesn't even have a couch."

"You're going to brush off a great guy because he doesn't have a sofa? Why don't you give him this damn couch? I've seen your storage space, and you have about five 'settees' too many." Uh-oh, Sophie was using air quotes.

"Look, I'm not saying that Nick's a forever guy. I don't think anyone's proposing marriage here. While you're looking for Mr. Forever, Nick could be Mr. Here and Now. Aren't you even attracted to him?"

Holly blushed to the roots of her hair. Thoughts of last night had her waving her hands to cool her heated face.

Sophie put down her spoon and smiled knowingly. "I may have to revise my theory on you and Nick going all the way last night. Look, all I'm saying is that he really likes you, and I think underneath all of that protesting, you like him too. It's rare for two people to have great chemistry, like you guys seem to have. I think you shouldn't give that up easily without at least pursuing it, seeing where it goes."

"Sophie, I don't want either one of us to get hurt. I'm probably a strong candidate for hooking up on the rebound. He's young and probably doesn't know any better."

"Then don't get hurt. No one says you have to lay your heart on the line. Young men have great stamina and short attention spans. If he can fill some of the lonely places you have in here," Sophie said nudging at Holly's heart, "let him."

After Sophie left, Holly knew she couldn't continue to dismiss Nick. He was hot. Her whole body tingled just thinking of him. There was no doubt about the chemistry they shared. She couldn't remember a man ever turning her on more. Plus, he was nice, considerate, and had been a really good friend when she needed one.

Throwing away the now empty container, Holly looked at the cordless phone on her kitchen counter. It was time to take the plunge and call Nick. She was tired of sleeping alone. He could definitely set the sheets on fire, and maybe a little bit of heat is what she needed.

If practice made perfect, she would enjoy perfecting her womanly arts with Nick. That way she'd know what to do with Mr. Right when she found him. As long as they knew the ground rules from the start, what was the worst that could happen?

Three

If Nick were physically able, he would have kicked himself in the ass. Standing in his living room, he looked down at the makeshift bed of rumpled throw pillows and blanket he and Holly had shared last night. He couldn't believe he'd totally blown it and let his dick rule his brain.

Holly had treated him like a horny teenager because he'd acted like a horny teenager. He was all over her the whole night. When he wasn't touching her, he was thinking about it. Any sane person walking into his house would have realized he had seduction on his mind.

Still, until Nick had come face to face with Holly as a free woman, he didn't know the depths of his feelings for her. His hope had been to see her at the party, talk to her, maybe see if his attraction to her was all in his mind.

Sometimes fantasy didn't meet up with reality after all. But with Holly, the reality was so much more. Seeing her alone on the deck, looking so vulnerable and lost, had been his undoing. He'd wanted to pull her into his arms right then and chase away whatever was making her blue.

When she'd walked through his front door, he felt like his house was finally a home. He hadn't realized her approval would mean so much to him. It was almost two years ago that his house had come on the market. He and his then girlfriend, Claire, were thinking of buying a place together—possibly taking their relationship to the next level, maybe a long engagement or marriage. But neither of them had been very interested in getting more serious, and when that became clear, they had gone their separate house-hunting ways.

Since Holly and Drew had spent two years looking for the perfect house, he had turned to her for advice—and her help had been invaluable. She'd helped him find a real estate agent, weed the good houses with great bones from termite ridden shacks, and had even accompanied him on the inspection with suggestions on how to negotiate the best possible price.

Then she and Drew had split, and Holly had gone into hibernation. He had understood that she needed time after her divorce, and he'd stood by, patiently waiting in the wings. All that anticipation, all that wanting had clouded his judgment on Saturday night. Her amber eyes flecked with need, all that curly dark hair spilling over his pillow. Her full, warm lips had called to him, and he had been unable to resist.

Nick shook his head, clearing the images from the night before. He was hard again, wanting her. He neatly stacked the large pillows against the wall and stored the throw blanket on a shelf under his giant screen TV, and dragged himself upstairs for a long shower. He set the water as cold as he could stand it.

Holly nearly jumped out of her skin when the phone rang. The caller ID read: Nick Andreis. Had her thoughts about him projected into the phone?

"Hello."

"It's Nick."

"I know."

There was a pause on the line. "I'm sorry about last night," he continued. "Can I come over? We need to talk."

"Sure," Holly said, and he instantly disconnected the call. Damn, I wouldn't have eaten that ice cream if I'd known Nick was coming.

Quickly brushing her hair and applying a little lip-gloss, Holly fidgeted on the couch, trying to look casual while her anticipation of Nick's visit built. Why was he sorry? Was he sorry that he had made love—and that's what it had been—with her? He'd gone from no regrets to sorry so quickly, he'd probably realized she was too old for him. Maybe he was coming by to put their relationship back in the "friend" zone.

When she heard the courtyard gate creak open and heavy footfalls on the stairs, Holly stood, took a deep breath, and rolled her shoulders like she'd been taught in yoga, trying to release the building tension.

She opened the heavy wood door before he knocked. Borrowing a little of Sophie's bravado, she decided to throw caution to the wind. Quelling the butterflies doing flip-flops in her belly, she took in the man who filled her doorframe. He looked good enough to eat, in a soft green, cashmere sweater that matched his eyes perfectly and fitted, tawny cords molded to his perfectly formed body.

"Hi," he said quietly.

Boldly, Holly grasped his hand, pulled him into her living room, and pushed the door closed. Looping her arms around his neck, she stood on her tiptoes and kissed him, releasing all her pent up desire she'd held back the night before. Holly knew with that move that she hadn't been drunk or fooling herself. There was chemistry between them she couldn't deny.

She nearly fainted as his tongue dueled with hers and his long hardness swelled against her belly. Ah, he felt it, too. Knowing where this might lead, Holly moaned wantonly. She was surprised when Nick unwound her hands from his neck and stepped back from her.

"Holly, this is not what I came here for."

Heat rushed to Holly's cheeks. God, what could she have been thinking? There was no way a young, virile guy like Nick would want to hook up with an aging cougar like her. She had just broken the cardinal rule of a one-night stand—even if they hadn't really made love in the traditional sense. He was probably coming to apologize and suggest they return to their pre-orgasmic relationship.

Nick shook his head then smiled almost wolfishly. "I want to talk to you about something else." He made his way to her antique, rolled-arm Edwardian settee and patted the space next to him. She sat primly, her feet tucked under her, girding herself for the inevitable let down.

"Can you spend the day with me on Friday?"

The unexpected question completely threw her off guard.

Impasse

"Sure… I guess they can get along without me at work for one day. Why?"

"There's something I want you to come see with me."

"Nick, I want to explain about my behavior just now… "

He shushed her with a finger to her lips, causing the same heady rush she got when his lips touched hers. "Please, don't say anything. I think we've already said too much today." He stood, pulling her with him, leaned down and gave her a chaste kiss on the cheek. "I'll be here to pick you up around ten o'clock. Okay?"

Holly nodded her agreement. Nick showed himself out. After Holly closed the door, she watched him from her picture window as he drove off What was she supposed to think now? Did he want her? Or want to let her down easy?

After all the convincing talk from Sophie, she had been very ready to give in to her desire to be with him despite their age difference, knowing he wasn't her forever guy. Instead, he was inviting her to spend time with him on Friday. Perhaps then they could get to the bottom of their attraction to each other. Maybe if they made love, or more likely had heart-stopping sex, she could work him out of her system and focus on finding Mr. Right.

On Friday morning, after calling work to wrap up a weekend Habitat for Humanity project staffed by Equia employees, Holly dressed in the most versatile clothes she could think of. She hadn't heard from Nick in four days, but he filled her thoughts nonetheless. She'd finally chosen a dark chocolate silk knit twin set, nipped at her waist, because it made her brown eyes more luminous. Tweed pants and low-heeled shoes completed her look.

Given California's casual style, she was dressed to go almost anywhere. If she could only figure out something to do with her hair. She was often mistaken for a teenager when her hair was down. The Shirley Temple curls always undid any elegance she was trying to achieve. But when she heard Nick's car pull up, Holly impulsively scraped her hair back into a quick chignon and slicked on some lip-gloss—no reason for Nick to think she wasn't trying.

Before Nick could come up, Holly grabbed her purse and ran down to meet him. The last thing she needed was another awkward situation where she came on to him and he turned her down. Even at her age, rejection was hard to take.

If he just wanted to be friends, it was fine with her. She loved her friends, and having one more good friend to count on was never a bad thing. Now, if she could just talk him into being friends with benefits, she thought smiling to herself, that would be even better.

Nick had just stepped out of his convertible and seemed surprised to see her in the courtyard.

Holly was walking toward the car, but Nick was walking toward her.

"Do you need something?" she asked, uncertain with him.

By way of an answer, Nick gathered her in his arms and kissed her full on the mouth. When other kisses would have ended, theirs changed. His mouth slanted against hers, his tongue sought entry and stroked hers.

Normally, Holly would have shied away from such a public display of affection. But propriety be dammed, Nick felt and tasted too good to let go. Her hand slipped under his sport coat to grasp his broad back. His lips and tongue teased hers, tasting of mint and wanting. Only their third kiss and she was addicted. When he unwound his arms from her waist, she grasped his hands.

"Nick?"

Nick saw Holly's confusion and wanted to kick himself again. He couldn't get this right to save his life. First he'd pawed her like a teenager, then he'd come over and blown her off after she'd come on to him—her kiss as sweet as ice cream.

Why couldn't he strike the right tone? He'd invited her out today so he could show her that there was more to his life than sex. He wanted a relationship with Holly, a real honest-to-goodness, boyfriend-girlfriend relationship with her. He wanted them to date, have dinner, watch movies, and, yeah, even have sex like any other couple would. Nick wished he could change how they'd come together on Saturday night, but he couldn't turn back the clock. He needed to move forward, and do it right this time.

"Holly, I just had to do that or the anticipation of kissing you would have distracted me all day, and my work would have been shot to hell." Nick rubbed a roughened thumb along her downy cheek. "I think we crossed wires the other day. I need you to know that I want you…desperately. I have wanted you for a very long time. That certainly hasn't changed from last weekend. I just hope that you want me, too."

Holly lowered her eyes. Then she nodded, almost imperceptibly. Nick took a deep, shuddering breath and shoved a hand through his hair.

"Then we better leave now before I abandon my crew and take you upstairs. But I promise you," he said, tilting her chin and looking her directly in the eye, "when I'm done with my work for today, I intend to do something about this."

Four

Nick put a hand on the small of her back and guided her toward the car. His touch branded her, creating tingles here, there, and everywhere his body came into contact with hers. Unable to articulate what she was feeling, Holly changed the topic once they were on the road.

"So, where are we going?"

While Nick masterfully guided the small convertible through L.A.'s late morning traffic snarl, she saw his disposition change. "We're going to the graduation of the Esperanza Nueva Charter High School."

"A commencement? In September?"

"It's an alternative charter school. Dean Callas can set any schedule he wants, so he holds classes year round. That way, he figures he can keep tabs on the kids, make sure they're engaged. He doesn't want them to have too much idle time. During their last summer, he helps them make college and career plans. He hopes that by holding graduation at the same time students are incoming, he can inspire the new kids—show them what they can achieve."

"This sounds like a wonderful place for kids."

"We think so. My partner, Helena and I have been working on a yearlong documentary—following the lives of students and families involved with the school."

"Wow, I didn't know you were working on this kind of project, or that you and Helena were partners now. I haven't seen her since she worked as Drew's assistant."

"I'm sure she'll be glad to see you. Helena loves this project as much as I do. And wait until you meet the kids, Holly. These young people come from some of L.A.'s toughest neighborhoods and the most challenging backgrounds, but they're striving, and they have hope for brighter futures."

On the drive, Nick explained more details of his documentary and what his crew would hope to capture today. A couple of years ago someone had invited him to the charter school's first graduation, and he'd been intrigued.

Nick had approached the school's director about following the students for a year, and the project was born. His production team picked seven different children to follow throughout their entire senior year at Esperanza Nueva. Not all the kids made it, but the sheer grit and determination of those who did would make a moving film. He and Helena planned to show the film at festivals, and if it found a distributor, major theaters around the country would show the documentary next year.

When they pulled up to one of the stately old churches that graced West Adams Boulevard, Nick quickly explained that the school lacked the adequate space for a ceremony of this size and scope. The church was impressive. It was a throwback to east coast grandeur incongruously surrounded by palm trees. He was looking forward to shooting in such a beautiful space and was assured it would lend the film a soberness not noted in other locations.

The parking lot was teeming with all shades of people, their faces suffused with happiness and pride. It was a picture of Los Angeles' diversity. Many of those same faces beamed with extra-wide smiles when they realized Nick was the man getting out of the car.

Many in the crowd reached for him and greeted him warmly. He returned those greetings, grasping some students' hands, hugging others. Holly, not wanting to spoil the moment, tried to slip quietly into the background, until Nick pulled her forward and introduced her to the crowd.

"Marco, Anthony, Carlos," he said to a few young boys, dressed in their Sunday best, at the front of the crowd, "I want you all to meet Holly. Make sure she meets everyone."

Surrounded by people suddenly patting her shoulder and giving her knowing winks, Holly felt about fifteen years old. When an older Hispanic woman pulled her aside, she gladly let herself be corralled.

"So, tell this old *abuela*, are you Nicky's *novia*?" she asked winking. "He's a good man. He's been a blessing to Esperanza—after seeing parts of his film, some well-to-do folks in Beverly Hills gave the school money and we will be able to buy new computers this year."

Holly was impressed with this side of Nick. He had always

been a "nice guy," but she had not realized the depths of his compassion.

After mingling with a number of students and parents and assuring them she was just Nick's friend, nothing more, Holly made her way to the church basement. Folding chairs faced the stage, where a single dais stood spotlighted.

The production crew lined up along the sides and against the back wall with lights and cameras poised to capture the stage activity and the onlookers' reactions. Although it was clear Nick was in charge, she noticed the camaraderie among the people he worked with. Toward the back, the heavenly smells of home-cooked meals presaged the reception afterwards.

A hush came over the crowd as a scratchy, well-worn CD started and the strains of Pomp and Circumstance filled the basement. Then, one by one, the graduates in their blue satin robes, mortarboards, and tassels marched down the makeshift aisle, their faces suffused with pride. More than one teenage mother walked down the aisle with her toddler in tow. Holly wished she had brought tissues when a young man, whom she had seen earlier in low-slung pants, now in a suit and tie under his gown, walked his mother down the aisle with him—both crying.

Unlike her own graduations with a single accomplished, well-known commencement speaker, each of the handful of students was able to speak about the struggles they'd overcome to get to today. The young graduates talked about overcoming drug addiction, gang violence, and coping with teen pregnancy. When the dean of the school handed out the diplomas, there wasn't a dry eye in the room. Toward the end of the ceremony, Holly was overjoyed when the students and the dean gathered on stage to read a short inspirational poem and award an honorary degree to Nick.

She was so proud of him, she thought she would burst. Drew had thought Nick was crazy for giving up on network television for documentaries and starting his own company, Solstice Entertainment. But Nick had followed his heart, and had obviously touched many others by doing so.

While Nick and a short, plump woman she recognized as Helena wrapped up their final interviews, Holly helped herself to the homemade delicacies. She enjoyed rice, beans, handmade tamales, and pupusas alongside the celebrating students and parents. She was in the middle of a conversation with a young girl about her own college alma mater when she felt Nick's presence just before his hand grasped her shoulder. His expression was blatantly sexual and all coherent thought fled. She pushed her card into the girl's hand, encouraging her to call about a possible internship at Equia, then stood and walked away with Nick.

"My crew is ready to wrap up here."

"You missed lunch. Do you want to go for a late bite?"

Nick smoothed an escaped tendril of hair behind her ear. "Holly, I'm not hungry for food right now."

His disheveled hair fell across his forehead partially covering his face, but she was still able to see the hunger radiating from his eyes. Suddenly, Holly felt very warm and hoped her face wasn't flushed with the desire that quickly overwhelmed her.

"Then let's get out of here," she said, feeling emboldened.

Nick grabbed her hand and swept her up the stairs and out the door before they could say any goodbyes. As they made their way north, Nick put the top down on the convertible, and Holly, already feeling carefree, took out most of the bobby pins and set her hair free. They drove swiftly through the busy streets until they reached stalled traffic at La Cienega Boulevard. Holly looked at the hills to the north imagining Nick's house somewhere up there.

"Nick, we have to talk," Holly blurted out before losing her courage to speak. He looked directly at her, the need smoldering in his eyes, and Holly almost lost her train of thought. "I… just want to make sure we lay some ground rules, so no one gets hurt." *So I don't get hurt.*

Nick broke eye contact as the traffic moved ahead a few feet.

Holly pressed on insistently. "Nick, we're obviously attracted to each other. I'm more crazy about you than I thought I would ever be about anyone again. I know that you're young and not interested in a serious relationship. So no strings attached. If you only want to spend tonight with me, I'll understand," Holly finished, hoping against hope that this craving for Nick, this wanting she hadn't known existed just a few days ago, could be assuaged after one night.

Nick didn't respond. The car's interior was intensely quiet as they followed the slow moving cars to her home. He was still silent when he pulled up to her building and helped her out of the car. Nick's nearness, coupled with his silence, kept Holly off balance. When they walked into her living room and Nick closed the door, she finally spoke into the awkward silence.

"Nick?"

Nick pulled her into his arms, his green eyes locking with hers.

Impasse

"Holly," he said, his voice gruff with need, "we can call it what you want. It can be however you like. None of that matters to me. More than anything, I want to be with you. No, I need to be with you. Now." He kissed her then, quelling all thought of a verbal response. His sensuous lips rubbed against hers, his tongue seeking and gaining entry.

The rationalizations and excuses that had been her constant companions for the last week flew from her head. Instead, she gave in to Nick's kiss and drowned in a world of sensation. She twisted fistfuls of Nick's ribbed sweater in her hands. Reluctantly breaking the kiss, she grabbed his hand and led him to her bedroom. Talking was done between them.

Even more than the rest of her apartment, Holly's bedroom was undeniably feminine— downright girly, to tell the truth. Her grandmother's mahogany canopy bed dominated the dark red room. Its gauzy curtains pulled aside revealing a pillowy lace duvet. Nick didn't look the least bit out of place in the frilly domain. He sat on the edge of the waist-high, "princess-and-the-pea" style mattress and pulled her between his strong thighs. Caught off balance at the sudden movement, Holly fell into his rock hard chest. Nick took advantage of her closeness to kiss her senseless.

Nick broke the kiss and looked at her, his eyes clouded with passion. When he spoke, his voice was hoarse with need and something far more compelling. "I've wanted this for so long," he said fiercely. He pulled at the few remaining bobby pins still holding the sides of her hair back, and her corkscrew curls spilled around her shoulders.

His words washed over her. Molten desire flooded Holly's

insides. Afraid of the depth of feeling radiating from Nick and the words spilling from his lips, Holly upped the distraction ante by boldly unbuttoning her cardigan and pulling her tank over her head. Nick's quick intake of breath as her see-through lacy bra came into view gave her the courage to continue.

Holly's hair curtained her face as she worked at the fasteners on her slacks, so she was unprepared for the feel of Nick's hot mouth wetting the lacy silk of her bra. Her nipples pulled hard under his skilled caress. She grabbed handfuls of his hair as he eased her bra straps down, and his mouth touched her flesh, his lips only grazing where she most wanted him to lick, to suck. She leaned forward to increase the contact, but Nick teased her, circling her areola with his tongue, then blowing on her overheated flesh. Holly felt achy all over—an ache, she now knew, only Nick could ease.

She pulled his sweater and t-shirt over his head. Holly unbuckled his belt and pulled it from the loops of his jeans. When she brushed her fingers against the hard ridge of his erection, he pulled her hands away and looped them around his neck.

"If you do any more of that, this will be over far too soon. I want to savor you."

Holly shivered at his provocative words. No man had ever made her feel so feminine, so wanted.

He stood, and they were skin to skin for the first time—her breasts crushed against the hard, muscled wall of his chest. Nick overwhelmed her—and if her heart weren't beating so fast or her womb weren't contracting with need, she would have put a stop to this madness that had ensnared her in a way she'd never imagined.

Impasse

Holly's loosened pants pooled at her feet, and she stepped out of them, along with her shoes. Clad only in black hipster panties, she stood before Nick. Desire, and something else she couldn't name, flared in his eyes as he looked his fill.

Reverently, he brushed her hair back over her shoulder. Nick's hands scorched fire down her arms. Caught in the intensity of his emerald gaze, Holly couldn't move, didn't want to move. His hands touched her everywhere, tracing her spine, palming the small of her back, glancing off her nipple, cupping her bottom. Holly was caught off guard when Nick effortlessly gathered her in his arms and laid her in the middle of her duvet. Never breaking eye contact, he shucked the rest of his clothes and lay beside her.

He was more beautiful than she had dreamed. Though she'd been too shy to look at him last weekend, she took him in greedily this time. Renovating his home had obviously agreed with him. There was not a spare ounce of flesh on his frame. His biceps were rock hard, his rippled stomach flat, his legs well muscled. She wanted to touch his golden skin and did. Holly impetuously straddled Nick's hips. She followed her sweeping hair across his body with her lips and tongue. She sucked at the strong column of his throat and flicked her tongue across his flat nipples. Tickling his belly button, Holly rubbed her cheek against his throbbing erection. It felt so hot, so hard.

When she stroked the underside of his penis, first with her lips, then with her tongue, Holly thought Nick would lose all control. "Oh, God, Holly, yes," he gasped. "Just like that… I've dreamed about this… but the reality… is so much more… " Taking him into her mouth, she sucked him as deep as she could, using the point of her tongue to taste the bead of moisture at the tip. Nick arched back and pulled her up, taking her mouth in another bone-melting kiss. He gently rolled himself on top of her, placing her on her back. His fingers found her center and stroked her clit, slipping inside and spreading the moisture there between her swollen folds. In an instant, their lovemaking went from a quiet coupling to frenzied mating. Holly tilted up to kiss him, their lips frantic, their tongues dueling. She laced her fingers in his hair and held on for dear life as he sucked one nipple, then pulled the other deep into his mouth.

The magical touch of his fingers brought her close to the edge, but she wanted to jump off that cliff into a sea of feeling with Nick right beside—no, inside her.

"Nick, please, I want you inside me." Holly sat up, pulling her nipple free from Nick's willing mouth. Grasping his cock at the base, she tried easing him in. There was a moment of hesitation as her body adjusted to fit his. They both sighed at the sweet perfection of their joining. Nick grasped her hips and helped her take him first slowly, her body accommodating his size as he filled her to the hilt, then faster as they both gasped for release. "Nick, don't stop. I'm so close," Holly said, feeling herself hover on the brink, the anticipation of her orgasm pooling in the pit of her stomach.

Following her verbal cue, Nick slid the pad of his thumb to her core and stroked her clit, slowly, and then faster, harder, as her cries escalated. Holly felt as if she were falling into a world of pure sensation and ecstasy. As she felt Nick's hot seed gush into her, she knew he had followed her over the edge.

With the exception of their labored breathing, the room was quiet. They remained joined for what seemed like an eternity

Impasse

while their bodies cooled. She couldn't believe how perfectly they fit. But Nick gently eased himself from her then padded to her bathroom. As the chill air in the room started to pucker her rapidly cooling flesh, Holly rolled over and scooted under her down duvet. When she moved, she felt warm and sticky. Then it hit her.

She and Nick had done the deed without a condom.

And she called herself the mature one. She had never been as caught up as she had been with Nick. Never had she allowed something like that to happen with anyone else, ever. When she heard Nick turning off the water in her bathroom, she called to him.

His frame filled the doorway to her bedroom, and she was hot all over again, despite the pit of worry that sat in her belly like a stone. Even unaroused, his penis was thick and heavy. He raked a hand through the hair that had fallen in his eyes, immodest despite his nudity. Holly shook herself, determined not to get distracted. She needed to be the adult in this situation. Sitting up, suddenly modest herself, she pulled the duvet up to her chin, and looked directly into his eyes still dark with desire.

"Nick…"

"Holly, let's not analyze what just happened between us," he said in that sexy baritone of his, sending chills down her spine.

"It's not that," Holly continued, more forcefully now. "We do need to talk because… well… you need to know, I'm not on the pill or anything. What just happened. We didn't protect ourselves."

Without a moment of hesitation, Nick strode purposefully to her bed and sat as close as her tucked covers would allow. "I'm clean, Holly. I don't want you to worry. I've been tested. I haven't been with anyone in a while."

"Nick, it's not that. I trust you," Holly said, though she was relieved Nick had thought of that while she was focused on a different aspect of their joining. "It's not that I think this will happen, not from this one time, but… "

He leaned forward, pushing back her hair, brushing his lips gently across hers and said, "We'll be more careful, I promise. I'll accept full responsibility for anything that happens. Anything."

Nick gently pulled the covers from her body and gathered her in his arms. When they made love this time, it was gentle and slow, and even more unnerving for Holly than their earlier frenzied coupling. When Nick entered her this second time, fully sheathed, she naively thought the impersonal latex barrier would somehow lessen the intensity of their union.

It was just the opposite. The deliberateness of Nick's caresses, the slow rhythm of their bodies magnified every action and made each stroke that much more meaningful. When their bodies quieted a second time, Nick fell into a deep sleep. Overwhelmed by what she and Nick had experienced, Holly felt the need to do something to distract her from her racing heart and mind. After pulling on matching velour shorts and hoodie over her bare skin, she tiptoed to the kitchen, sure not to wake him, and turned on the oven to pre-heat.

Nick awoke with the smell of chocolate chip cookies surrounding him. Something else he couldn't name filled the night air. Was it mint? He pulled on his boxer briefs with some difficulty, already half hard, thinking the third time with

Impasse

Holly tonight would definitely be a charm.

She was languorously stirring something on the stove when he entered the kitchen. Slightly startled, Holly looked up. Nick took in the woman he'd pined for before speaking. She had pulled her hair into a loose ponytail, but a few escaped tendrils kissed her cheeks—rosy from the heat. The hip hugging tan velour shorts she wore barely covered her slim, shapely legs, reminding him how her limbs had felt wrapped around his hips as he plunged into her again and again, just hours earlier.

"What are you doing?"

"Wait, I'm almost done." She poured the liquid into tall glass mugs and put them on a tray. "I was going to bring this to you. Go back to bed and pretend to be surprised."

Nick made a mock run for the bedroom, where Holly put the loaded tray on her nightstand and pounced on top of him. The cookies, which had seemed so appetizing moments before, were forgotten as he kissed her. He unzipped her hoodie halfway, dying for a peek at her pink-brown nipples.

Were they were already hard or would he have to help stimulate her flesh? She stroked his erection through his underwear as he grazed her nipple with his teeth. Then she pulled away.

"I'm hungry… for food," she breathed a little unsteadily.

They shifted their attention from fulfilling their need for each other, for the moment, to filling their empty stomachs. Nick bit into a soft chocolaty cookie and took a sip of what turned out to be mint infused hot chocolate. "Mmmm, did you make these from scratch? How long was I asleep?"

"Yes, they're homemade. You weren't asleep that long. I keep ingredients on hand for nights when I have chocolate cravings."

The cookies were divine. Holly was divine. Sitting up against the headboard, Nick grew thoughtful. He knew he needed to tell her how much this meant to him: she was more than a one—or two-night stand.

"Holly, I… this is more amazing than I ever hoped. I've been thinking about being with you for the last year, at least. All these months, I've been dreaming about you, wanting you. I think—"

Holly quieted him by placing trembling fingers to his lips. "Shhhh. It's too much too soon." Her eyes skittered away. The mood in the room shifted perceptibly. "You know, it's getting kind of late. Do you mind? I'd like to sleep alone tonight."

Nick started to say something about the abrupt change in her mood, but her shuttered look silenced him.

"I have to, you know, brush my teeth." She excused herself, and by the time she returned from the bathroom, he'd done what she asked. He'd pulled on his clothes and had readied himself to leave. When Holly stood on her tiptoes and kissed him on the cheek, he gave in to the urge to pull her in tight. When her startled gaze met his, he kissed her full on that pouty little mouth. It was a full minute before she pulled back, out of breath.

It was another minute before she recovered. "Sleep tight," she trilled with false gaiety, ushering him out the door. "No strings, remember. Let's get together soon when we both have time."

He could tell it took a lot for her to push him through the door.

Holly sagged against the heavy door, glad she'd been able to get him out. The sex was good, too damn good. She didn't want to hear anything serious, not from him, not now. Why did he have to ruin a perfectly good time?

Looking at him, sensing what he was thinking, what he wanted to say made Holly jittery down to her very fingertips. This wasn't what she'd bargained for. After he'd awoken, everything about his demeanor screamed relationship with a capital R. She just wasn't ready to go there, not with him, not now.

When she finally heard his car start, she started making her way to clean up the kitchen. She picked up the ringing telephone. The cookie sheet would have to wait.

"Are you alone?" Sophie wasn't big on social niceties, like greetings.

"I live alone."

"I got a dog. You'll have to come meet Sasha."

Holly was thrown by the unexpected news. "Were you planning to get a dog?"

"Nope." Sophie related a long and bizarre story about her and some strange man saving a dog from certain death on the Hollywood freeway.

The guy sounded more intriguing than the dog. "Who's the guy? Did he want the dog?"

"He was just some suit. I put first rights on Sasha and I got her. Easy peasy. She's really cute. Maybe you should get a dog, since you seem to be A-L-O-N-E. Where's Nick? I thought you had afternoon plans." Sophie started humming something out of tune.

"What song is that?"

"'Love in the Afternoon.' It was a song from a movie with Hepburn and Cooper. Did you get any?"

Holly could feel heat creeping from her neck to her cheeks.

"Nick and I… may have."

The sound of clapping hands came through the receiver. "Congratulations. Did he have work to do?"

"Um, no. I don't think so." Holly answered. It was sometimes hard to keep up with Sophie.

"So where the hell is he? I IM you, I text, I call, and he's never there."

Holly's mood sobered. "I kind of kicked him out."

"What the fuck?"

"If you must know, the sex was great. You were right about getting back out there, but he started talking about feelings and this, whatever we're doing—did—is not about that."

"Not about what?"

"You know where I am. It's no secret. I want marriage, kids, the whole nine yards."

"And Nick wants a relationship. Relationships lead to marriage. I feel like I missed something."

"He's not right for me, now. Plus, you know I have rules."

"Rules, schmules. Are you going to see him again, or did you toss him out for good?"

The thought of not seeing Nick again made Holly's heart hurt. "I don't know."

Sophie's disagreement was obvious from all the sighing and harrumphing. But the dog started barking. Sophie had to get off the phone, and couldn't harass her anymore.

Holly went back to cleaning the kitchen. Next she attacked the bedroom, pulling the sheets from the bed. It had taken all her strength and resolve to send Nick packing after what they'd shared that afternoon. But, she needed some time alone.

Impasse

It was times like these that she wished her grandmother were alive to give her sage advice. Her brain was screaming for her to get Nick out of her life now. Her body, and her heart were a different matter. He could be so much more than a one or two night stand. If only he were older, more settled, he might be just the person to fill the lonely space in her heart.

Five

Nick lied. Maybe it wasn't so much a lie but more of an omission. If Holly thought their relationship would have no strings, then so be it. He had waited this long. He could wait some more. He could show the patience of Job. After being with her last night, he wanted her for keeps. He had been more than halfway in love with her for the last year or so. Their last two "dates" and had pushed him over the edge.

What had him racking his brain was figuring out how to convince her that he wasn't one of the commitment phobic, hook-up-with-girls-today-leave-them-crying-tomorrow players she associated with people in his generation. With no immediate solution in mind, Nick called his father. Maybe if they got some work done on the house, he'd feel better.

Nick helped his dad carry up five-gallon drums of paint, rollers, and an extra ladder. He would not think about Holly. He would not think about Holly. He'd think about painting his bedroom.

"So, Nicky, you gotta tell me. Why the change in color?" Dominic Andreis asked, his Chicago accent thick despite his years in southern California. "The guys at the paint store were laughing their asses off when I told them it was for my son's bedroom."

Dominic was an old school kind of guy. He'd been a contractor all of his life and was a man's man all the way through. Nick could see how his dad had some questions about this sudden shift from a manly navy to a less masculine crimson bedroom. He didn't answer the question. Instead, he asked his own once they had settled into a good painting rhythm.

"Dad, how did you convince Mom to marry you?"

Nick missed his mother. He didn't really talk about her much with his Dad because the topic clearly pained the older man. Nick's mother, Iris, had been every child's dream. She'd always been there for him and his siblings. It had been devastating to all of them when she got sick and died unexpectedly of pancreatic cancer. It was one of the reasons, Nick thought, that his father had sold their childhood home, and everyone had scattered around the globe.

"Whoa, ho," Dominic said, and raised his eyebrows knowingly. "Ahh, all this is about a girl. Now I understand the sudden need to work on the house this weekend. You think she'll like this color?"

"She's not a girl. She's very much a woman, Dad."

"Sorry, can't keep up with the newfangled lingo." Dominic smiled, but his eyes became more serious as he thought about his wife. "Iris almost didn't marry me."

Nick was taken aback. "But I thought you guys were childhood sweethearts."

"We never told you the whole story because you didn't need to know." Dominic paused. "Maybe now you do."

"So, what happened?" Nick asked impatiently, his roller slipping sideways, marring the wet paint.

"Pay attention to what you're doing, Nicky. You can paint and listen at the same time," his father admonished.

Nick, sighed, picked up a brush, and began fixing the small mistake he had made.

"Like I've always told you, we met in junior high. I proposed to her during our senior year at , but she turned me down.

"Your grandpa didn't want an Italian girl like her marrying an Orthodox Greek guy like me—culture clash and all that. So I moved out here to apprentice with your uncle Alessandro, and forget about her. No matter how many dances I went to, or girls I dated, I could not get your mother out of my mind. A couple years later, I heard that she had gotten engaged.

"After a lot of bluster on my part about how I would speak now and never hold my peace at her wedding, Alex and I drove back to Chicago in a used 1946 Plymouth Deluxe—I'll never forget that car—and we busted up her wedding. Your mom and I eloped the next day, and the rest, as they say, is history.

"It took a number of years, after you and your brother and sister were born, for her parents to forgive me. But I loved her. She never had to work. I made a good living for us until the day she died, God rest her soul."

"I never knew this," Nick said, truly understanding for the first time how deep his parents' love must have been.

Impasse

"Nicky, the bottom line is, if you love her, go after her," Dominic said with a twinkle in his eye. "Now, when do I get to meet this little filly?"

Nick hesitated a moment. "You've already met her."

"You haven't brought any girls around since your mom died. I think I would have noticed a pretty, young thing hanging about. I may be old, but I'm not quite dead."

"You met her a couple of years ago at her house on Thanksgiving. Her name is Holly Bu—um, Prentice."

"Is it that girl with the crazy colored hair and all those earrings?"

"I've told you before Dad, that's Sophie. Holly's the one with the beautiful, curly hair. She cooked, remember?"

"But isn't she married to that uptight entertainment exec, Andrew something?" His father scowled at what he could only assume were Nick's adulterous thoughts. "You got the part of the story where I rescued your mom before she was married to another guy, right?"

"Dad, you raised me better than that. She separated from Drew two years ago. They've been divorced about a year."

Dominic nodded, his memory jogged. "I liked her, Nick—boy, could she cook. If you're sure, then you should go after her. Life is too short not to be with the woman you love." Finished with the first coat of the deep red paint, they descended the ladders. "Now, maybe she'll take you seriously if you cut your hair," Dominic said as he playfully ruffled his son's paint-flecked strands.

"I think she likes the hair just fine, Dad," Nick said blushing, remembering her grabbing his hair, more than once, in the heat of their passion.

"So, tell me, kiddo, what kind of plan do you have? I don't want any man in our family ruining another wedding."

Six

"I'll be over in half an hour," he said, his voice crackly through his cell phone.

"Okay," Holly said brightly. "I'm looking forward to it." She hung up the phone and checked herself in the mirror again. Except for Nick, because their last two encounters certainly didn't count, Holly hadn't been on a date in more than six years.

After going back and forth in her mind what seemed like a thousand times, Holly had decided to take the plunge and start dating again. If Nick had done anything for her, he'd freed her from her two-year bout of celibacy. Her girlfriends were right. Sophie was right. It was time to move on from being the victim of her divorce. She wasn't the first woman to have her marriage unexpectedly crumble, and she couldn't let it keep her down forever.

Nick was great. Really great, if she were being honest with herself, but not long-term relationship material. If her goal was permanency, to settle down, she needed to look at more suitable, age appropriate, marriageable candidates. Ryan Becker, her date tonight, certainly fit the bill.

Smoothing down the well-fitted caramel-colored shirtdress she knew complimented her golden eyes, Holly opened the door when she heard heavy footfalls on the tile stairs. She quickly closed the door behind her to avoid the awkwardness of feeling obligated to invite him in for a drink.

"Ryan, it's good to see you," Holly said, hugging him in greeting. Holly tried her darnedest not to compare Ryan to Nick as she broke the embrace. He was taller and stockier than Nick. Styled blond hair surrounded his boyish face, and ocean blue eyes gave him that classic California surfer look.

Looking beyond her toward the door of her apartment, he asked, "Do you need anything else or are you ready to go?"

"I'm ready," Holly said,, shouldering her bag and gathering the tissue thin, fringed cashmere wrap around her shoulders.

All chivalry and politeness, Ryan escorted her downstairs, guiding her by the small of her back. He opened the passenger door of his sleek new Acura TL and helped her in. Holly belted herself in to the car, admiring the sleek buttery leather, as Ryan got into the driver's side. It was just the kind of car she would expect a lawyer to have, obviously expensive but not too ostentatious.

"I hope you like the restaurant," he said, and Holly thought she heard the faintest quiver of nerves in his voice. She felt for him because she wasn't nervous at all. Her main goal was to enjoy herself and not think about Nick with his model good looks, his kindness, how he made her feel when the lights went out.

"I'm sure I'll like it fine," Holly said, refocusing her thoughts

Impasse

back on the man at hand. To help dispel his nervousness, she filled the car with chatter about the project where they had met. Even though Ryan had worked as an attorney at Equia for years, Holly had only met him a year ago when she needed some help on a contract with a non-profit agency. He'd advised her on that project and, because they got along so well, they shared coffee at the commissary on more than one occasion.

She'd been surprised several months later when he'd shown up one Saturday to help her on a community project. He was a nice, single guy who seemed to be interested in her, if his not-so-subtle mentions of dinner were any indication. So, she finally accepted an invitation for a bona fide date.

She was curious when they made their way southwest to Culver City near the studio and not the usual restaurant meccas of Beverly Hills or Santa Monica. Culver was a small city surrounded by the larger metropolis of Los Angeles. It had once been the heart of the early century movie industry, the home of classics like the Wizard of Oz. After many of the studios had moved to Burbank and surrounding areas in the San Fernando Valley, seeking acres of space in the sunny climate, only Equia and a couple of other industry players remained nearby. Despite that, the city had recently gone through a renaissance and many new restaurants and night clubs had located in the downtown area. They pulled up to the valet in front of a restaurant Holly knew to be owned by the son of a major A list action star.

Of course, Ryan had conscientiously made reservations, and without delay they were escorted to a quiet corner booth in an otherwise raucous restaurant, filled with the lingering happy-hour crowd from the nearby studios.

Sipping the apple-cinnamon old fashioned she'd ordered, Holly set her mind to getting to know Ryan better and forgetting Nick, for at least a few hours.

"So, tell me, what brought you to Los Angeles?" Holly asked, smiling and leaning forward, acquitting herself like a woman on a first date should. After all, Ryan was a perfectly nice guy.

Ryan explained that he'd always wanted to work in the entertainment industry. That and strong family ties had lured him back to the City of Angels after a long stint in school back east. As they worked their way through Tuscan style flattened chicken and smoked trout salad, she realized that Ryan was the perfect marriage candidate. He enjoyed his work; he was a couple of years older than her and talked about being ready to settle down. In a perfect world, she should be ready to walk down the aisle with a guy like this—in a heartbeat.

Yet the evening was a disaster.

She sipped from her wine glass and pushed around her uneaten dinner, gathering her courage.

"Hey there," she said softly, stopping him in the middle of a sentence. "I can see this isn't going anywhere between us. What's really on your mind tonight?"

Ryan closed his blue eyes briefly. "I met someone."

Holly's release of breath was audible. "That's such a weight off my shoulders. I met someone, too. Well not exactly someone new, but I'm sort of involved with someone I've known for a long time, though I don't think I want to be," she said shaking her head. "Sorry, that was probably too much information. Tell me about the woman you met."

"I met this woman. I can't… get out of my mind."

Impasse

"What's she like?" Holly said, really focusing on what Ryan was saying for the first time that evening. Maybe she could give him advice about his budding romance. She obviously didn't understand a thing about men. But women, she knew.

"She's nothing like me. It was like a breath of fresh air. I met her in the craziest way. We were trying to save this dog on the freeway—"

Holly interrupted before he could finish his thought. "You're talking about Sophie? My best friend, Sophie Reid?" she asked, suddenly feeling more energetic than she had been anytime that night. This was the most bizarre coincidence.

"I didn't exactly get her name."

"Well how would you describe her?"

"She's about five-foot three or four with yellow—no, now I think it's red—hair and a sunflower yellow Volkswagen Beetle with this clever vanity plate."

"EW A BUG," they said together, laughing.

"That's definitely Sophie," she said. Still, this didn't bode well. Sophie went out a lot, but didn't date any one guy more than a few times. Lawyers were on the top of her "never" list. If Sophie weren't so stubborn, Holly thought they might actually be good together. "Are you guys—um—seeing each other?" she asked politely, though the answer was obvious.

"She won't see me," he said soberly. "I'm pretty sure there's something between us. I mean, on the surface we don't have much in common, but I'm still intrigued."

"Mmm, she doesn't date lawyers, you know," Holly said, hedging. She was not a meddler. "It's kind of a bright line rule with her."

"Why?"

"I don't feel comfortable disclosing that," Holly said. She didn't want to get into Sophie's family issues or hang-ups. "That's something she should explain to you herself, I think."

"I don't exactly know how to contact her," Ryan protested, taking on a lost little boy look that she imagined most women couldn't help but find endearing. "Can you give me her number at least?"

Holly wasn't the least bit affected by his plea. Best friends were good at sticking together. "I'm sorry, I thought I heard someone's voice," she said, looking over to the bar crowded three-deep. The wavelike movement of the people at the bar distracted her for a long moment before she turned back to the table.

"Ryan, I don't think I'd feel comfortable going against her wishes like that," she said firmly. "I can tell you that she's helping me do some volunteer work at the Korby Center next weekend."

"The Korby Center?"

"You know I organize volunteer events for Equia, right? Well I've had a little problem getting volunteers for this event next weekend. We're supposed to landscape and redecorate a residential home for foster kids who've aged out of the system."

"Oh, I saw that in last month's Otter newsletter. It seems worthwhile. I'm surprised more people from work didn't volunteer."

"Well, it's not too late to add yourself to the list. We can always use more volunteers. Plus, I guarantee Sophie will be there."

He nodded, smiling once again. "I'd love to help you out."

Holly chuckled. "I'm sure the Korby kids will appreciate your altruism. I'll email you the details." She studied his crisp tailored clothes. He was a "suit" through and through. Maybe Sophie could loosen him up. "Oh, and you should dress down… way down."

Great. Now she was hearing voices. No matter how hard she tried, Holly could not shake her thoughts of Nick. It had been like this all week. A baritone voice breaking out from the crowd, a sudden laugh. Every single time it was like time stood still. She turned around in circles, looking, expecting to hear his happy greeting. It was utterly distracting. Tonight was no different. She could only pay partial attention to Ryan. Nick so filled her thoughts, she was sure she heard his voice even as she and Ryan finished up with caffè lattes, and prepared to leave.

Ryan, his hand lightly at her waist, helped her weave through the tables, even more packed by the Friday night crowd than when they entered. Holly heard Nick's voice again then did a double take. It was actually him this time, not her imagination. There he was, leaning against the bar sharing an after-work drink with what she surmised were friends from the studio.

As if she had called his name, he turned and saw her. Their eyes locked before his slid right to notice Ryan. Holly thought she saw a flash of anguish in his wince, but she ignored it. She wasn't prepared to deal with what her actions did to Nick. He put down his drink. After a very brief conversation with a couple of his friends, he strode over to them.

"Can we talk for a second?" Nick demanded without any fanfare.

Sensing that the conversation they were about to have was for their ears only, Ryan took that opportunity to step outside. "I'll just arrange things with the valet. See you in a few minutes."

"What's going on?" Nick pressed.

"There's nothing going on. Or everything. I don't know. My friends suggested I start dating, seriously, again. So here I am on a date with Ryan."

"Is that his name?" Nick asked, his jaw clenched in an obvious attempt not to grind his teeth.

"Yes, Nick. That's his name," she explained as if she were speaking with a stubborn toddler. "I don't know why you're so angry. We decided that our situation has no strings."

"You decided, Holly. You. That would not be my choice. I've never denied that I want you. All of you."

But for how long? Holly asked herself, wisely keeping that question to herself. Nick drew closer, obliterating the sight of others in the restaurant. He leaned his left arm against the wall behind her, shielding her from the rest of the bar and restaurant patrons. With their intense focus on each other, the sound receded as well. He grasped her hand in his.

"What do you want me to do?" she asked.

"I can't deal with the idea of you seeing other people. Can we just be monogamous while we're together, no matter how long that is?" When Holly didn't respond, Nick pulled his car keys from the front pocket of his form fitting jeans. "Come home with me now. We need to talk about this."

"Nick, I don't know if there's anything else to say." Her eyes flickered in the direction of the front door. "Plus, I'm on a date here." Holly whispered, lowering her voice so it was barely audible as Ryan approached. "I owe it to him to see this night through."

Ryan cleared his throat, overhearing them anyway. Nick dropped his hands and stepped back from Holly, their intensity broken. "Holly, you don't owe me a thing. I had a very nice time, but it looks like you have your hands full. So I'll see you at work sometime," he said graciously. To Nick, he said, "You're a really lucky guy. Make sure you get her home safely." With that, he turned on his heel and headed toward the line of shiny late model cars the valets had lined up for patrons leaving the restaurant.

It was two long, deserted blocks to Nick's car, parked in one of the studio lots. They covered the ground in electrically charged silence. The drive back to his place was as quiet as their short walk had been. Holly shifted uncomfortably in the seat and stared out the window to avoid making eye contact with him. Nick didn't seem exactly happy, and part of her was starting to feel guilty, but for what, she didn't know.

Reluctantly, Nick pulled his eyes away from Holly. He wished he knew what she and that Ryan guy were talking about so intently, their heads bent together. Though her "date" tonight with Ryan didn't seem too serious if the guy was willing to leave so quickly. He shook his head. The guy didn't even put up a fight. He wasn't good enough for her.

Nick needed to pay attention to the road. But she looked fucking incredible. It stuck deeply in his craw that she'd dressed up for another man. The dress molded to her pert breasts and her curvaceous bottom, leaving little to the imagination. She had dusted her skin with some kind of powder that made it shimmer in the moonlight, giving her an ethereal glow.

Nick wanted nothing more than to unbuckle her belt, pop her buttons, and feast upon the delicate flesh. Even if a committed relationship were out of the question, he knew that monogamy was not up for debate. He'd never thought of himself as particularly possessive, but the idea of sharing her made him feel downright murderous.

"Come with me," Nick said, holding out his hand after parking the car in the garage.

"Nick?" Holly said questioningly, shrugging awkwardly.

"Holly, we're adults, and inside my house is the best place to sit right now and talk this out."

She looked wary, but took his hand.

Inside, Nick removed the purse and scarf from her hand and dropped them unceremoniously next to the cold hearth. Abandoning conversation, and not waiting for an invitation, Nick leaned Holly against the wall and kissed her, releasing the passion that had bottled up for the last week. The kiss was hard, sexy, passionate—his tongue sought and gained entry. Holly hesitated only for a second before giving into his heat.

Pulling back from the kiss, he leaned his forehead against hers. The echo of their heavy breathing was the only sound in the almost empty room. More than the physical, which he could see, hear, feel, Nick craved verbal confirmation that his feelings weren't one sided.

"Do you feel what's happening between us?"

Nick did not wait for an answer. Instead, he cupped her bottom and lifted her to his hips. Holly's legs reflexively wrapped around his waist—her center meeting the ridge of his straining erection. He needed to show her how it was for him. Looping her hands tightly around his neck, seeking his mouth, Holly only nodded in response to his question.

Nick acceded to her silent entreaty and kissed her. When he

broke the kiss a second time, he carefully carried her upstairs and deposited her on the king size bed, her hair spilling over the footboard. He didn't turn on the bedside lamp. He could see all he needed to in the moonlight that caressed her glowing skin.

Nick finally gave in to his desire to unbuckle the wide belt that encircled her small waist and undo the gold buttons that fastened the tiny dress she wore. He almost lost control right then when he realized she wore the sheerest lingerie he had ever seen. The filmy gold fabric did little to hide her erect nipples or the dark triangle of hair that covered her sex. He only wished she'd dressed this way to entice him and him only.

All thoughts of anyone other than Holly flew out of his mind when he felt her small fingers deliberately grasp his penis through his jeans. Even with layers separating her hand from his pulsing flesh, her touch almost sent him through the roof. All bets were off. He suckled at one nipple through the silk of her bra while his hand strayed below the band of her gold thong, touching the dampened curls. Her mewling cries spurred him on to stroke her.

His fingers parted her nether lips and stroked the hardened bud he found there, while he pulled the bra away from her breast with his teeth and gently bit her nipple. She bucked, and her hands frantically pulled at his belt, his button fly jeans, and his boxer briefs until she reached the heart of him. He alternated between licking, biting, and blowing on her engorged nipples, all the while stroking her clit.

"Nick," she cried out. "I can't hold back, I'm going to come."

Nick didn't stop, didn't let up. "I want you to melt for me."

And melt she did. Her legs held his hand in a vice like grip as spasms rolled over her in waves. When her moans subsided, Nick shucked his own clothes and sheathed himself in a condom from his bedside drawer.

"Oh God, that feels so good," Holly moaned as he filled her.

Interlacing their fingers above her head, Nick slowly thrust into her, then retreated.

"You're so unbelievably tight," he breathed. "You fit me like a glove. It's so… perfect."

He looked down at her, lit by the moon. Her small breasts quivered with each thrust, the nipples beaded. She bit her full bottom lip, tossing her head from side to side. He had to have her for more than just tonight. Watching her, being inside her, the stimulation was so intense he could feel his balls quiver. It took everything he had not to come right away. When Holly wrapped her feet, still clad in those sexy strappy, golden sandals, and her yoga toned legs around his waist, it changed the angle of their joining. He lost all control. He pistoned into her and she met him thrust for thrust. When her internal muscles quaked and milked him, he let go, and she came a second time, their cries mingling in the still air.

When Holly reached to turn on the only bedroom lamp, Nick grabbed her hand. He wasn't ready for her to see the color of the room. It revealed more than he wanted to share just then. He was thinking long term. But she was acting like a scared rabbit and he didn't want her hopping away in fright now that he had her here.

"Leave it for now. I like to look at the lights in the hills."

Holly tentatively scooted to the far edge of the mattress and leaned against the headboard. Nick sat naked and cross-legged on the bed, facing her, the nighttime shadows dancing across her face.

"Look, I'm not going to beat around the bush. I want to see you, Holly, more than once every few weeks or days."

"Nick, we've gone over this. I'm not ready for a relationship. You're too young, and I've seen too much of the world," she protested. "You're a really nice guy and all that, but I don't know if we should continue to see each other."

Nick ran a single finger down the soft skin of her arm. Holly shivered, her nipples standing to attention.

"Your body says different."

Holly pulled the duvet over her knees and under her chin in an apparent effort to hide her traitorous breasts from his gaze.

Nick brushed her hair behind her ears and shoulder. "You don't have to hide yourself from me, Holly."

"I don't think we should be together if we don't have plans for anything long term. I don't want to just pass the time. I really need to start working on my future," Holly said.

"What future are we talking about?" Nick asked, trying to keep a pleading note out of his voice. "Why can't I be a part of that future?"

"We've been over this before. You're twenty-six. I was already in first grade when you were born. We didn't grow up watching the same shows, listening to the same bands. Here's a good one: My prom song was a Whitney Houston's 'I Will Always Love You.' What was yours?"

Nick had the good sense to act abashed. "I think it was some Britney Spears song," he said with a wry smirk.

Holly rolled her eyes. "It's not just those trivial differences, Nick. I've been married and divorced. I want to be married again—'til death do us part' this time. I want children, to grow old with someone. The usual things women my age think of when we hear the biological clock ticking."

"But you can't deny our chemistry. That has to be good for something. Give us this chance, Holly," Nick said. He surreptitiously crossed his fingers out of her line of sight. "We should be able to work out this hunger for each other. Give us until Thanksgiving at least. That's all I ask."

Holly wanted to agree; he could see it in her downcast eyes. She nodded almost imperceptibly. He grabbed her free hand in a fierce grip, triumphant.

"We have to see eye to eye on very specific ground rules, Nick." He half expected her to pull out a lined pad and paper, except, like him, she was naked.

"I couldn't agree more," Nick said. "The first rule we have to establish is that we're monogamous for as long as we're together. I can't tolerate you seeing anyone else."

"Okay," Holly agreed, slowly. He hoped she couldn't imagine sharing him with anyone either.

"What else, Holly? I'll do whatever you want to make this work."

"No staying over. I prize my alone time now. I don't want either of us feeling obligated to stay the night. No reason pretending it's something it's not."

Crossing his index and middle fingers even tighter behind him, Nick agreed to that condition. Subsequently, he also agreed not to talk about feelings and not to discuss the future. Except for the monogamy rule, he did not intend to follow any of them. But to be with Holly, to get her to consider being with him for keeps, he'd do anything to have the time to convince her that they could be right for each other in many more ways than just in bed.

Seven

Phone calls weren't against the rules. It was a huge oversight on her part. Holly didn't have to check the caller ID to know it was Nick when the phone rang at nine-thirty on the third Friday night in October. She'd never thought a man could affect her so deeply without even being in the room.

Every single night after her abandoned date, without fail, Nick called. It was as if he were a devoted boyfriend, not her interim lover. Sometimes when he called, they would talk about her day. Other times, he would ask about her work. The most difficult conversations for Holly were when he would ask about her hopes and dreams. Every time Nick talked about the future—his, not theirs, she had to remind herself—Holly felt like a fraud.

If Nick were her Mr. Right instead of her Mr. Right Now, she would welcome his attention. Who didn't want a man who wasn't commitment phobic? But with someone who was only temporary, the last thing Holly wanted was to rely on him, get used to him, need him, if he was only there for sex in the moment.

Almost daily, Holly struggled to strike the right balance between friends and lovers when she and Nick were together, or even when they weren't. More and more it seemed Nick acted like theirs was a traditional boyfriend/girlfriend relationship, after they had both agreed it wasn't going to be like that. When she felt Nick was getting too close, she'd invite him over and screw his brains out. It always distracted him from any kind of deeper or more meaningful conversation. Who could discuss feelings during a screaming orgasm? Still, a once great friendship now tinged with hot, sweaty sex disconcerted Holly.

"Hi, Nick," Holly spoke into the phone late one night by way of greeting.

"Holly, did you work out that problem with the Korby Center?"

She should not have been surprised that he remembered. She was learning that he was that kind of guy. For weeks, she had been having trouble recruiting volunteers for her company's project at the not-for-profit Korby Center. And D-Day was tomorrow.

Because Korby's board of trustees had already publicized the project in their donor newsletter, Holly now felt more obligated than usual to live up to Equia's reputation as a generous community donor. One of Korby's trustees had even confided in Holly that their donations had skyrocketed when their benefactors found out Equia was working with the center. The volunteer effort had to be successful.

"I've enlisted the president to send out an email requesting volunteers. I think there's a good chance that we'll get a bunch of people that way—though I haven't gotten many people on the email invite."

"I know it will work out," Nick said. "You can count on me if you need an extra hand. I'm sure I could also recruit a few kids at Esperanza Nueva. The dean there is always encouraging the students to give back to the community."

"I may take you up on that," Holly said. Switching gears, her voice became throatier when she asked, "Do you want to come over now?"

There was a pause on the line. For a moment, Holly worried, as she did every time they spoke, that he may reject her overture, that the time before was the last time; but then Nick spoke again, his voice as husky as hers. "I'll be over in about a half hour," he growled into the telephone before she heard it clatter into its base.

"See you then," Holly said to dead air, then disconnected the call.

She waited but pretended not to wait for him. Showing him her naked desire made her feel vulnerable—and pretending not to want, not to crave him, was the easiest way she could think of to protect her heart. Today her disguise was in the form of a woman's magazine.

While the minutes ticked by, she mindlessly flipped through the magazine, skipping the articles on how to catch a man—she had one man too many, by her count—and how to have multiple orgasms, since that wasn't a problem with Nick. In exactly thirty minutes, not one second later, Nick's car door shut with a resounding thud. She looked up from her magazine, feigning disinterest, in case he could see her through the living room window.

Damn, he looked good enough to eat. He was wearing the

sexy-as-hell bomber jacket she loved over a trendy, tight-fitting thermal that only emphasized his sculpted chest. The well-worn jeans, thinning in all the right spots, molded to his frame, leaving little to her imagination.

She had thought their "relationship" would have petered out by now. Surely, there were hordes of twenty-something hotties he would like to get with, waiting in the wings. But if there were, he didn't seem interested. Not that she could blame him, because she hadn't fully dedicated herself to her dating project either—finding her Mr. Right, a guy ready to settle down with her, have a family.

They had agreed on monogamy, but if she found the perfect guy… well, her biological clock was ticking. It was just that right now, the sound was muted by her desire for Nick. Being with Nick felt so wonderful, she wasn't ready to give him up quite yet. Maybe in another three weeks, or three months, they'd be ready to go their separate ways. The smoldering look in Nick's sage green eyes told her tonight wasn't going to be the night they called it quits.

Before she could close the door, his hand caught in her hair. Their mouths fused, seeking release in one another. When they broke apart to catch their breath, Holly vaguely registered the duffel bag Nick dropped on her living room floor as he pushed her door shut.

All she could think of was how quickly she could remove his clothes and get him to her bedroom. Though they had been together three nights that week already, their coupling was still frenzied, full of savage hunger. She couldn't get enough of him to fill her.

Impasse

While he unzipped her cashmere cardigan, she pushed his jacket from his shoulders, molding her hands to the rock hard muscles of his chest, shoulders, and back. She gasped when his hands cupped her breasts, unfettered under her thin tank. They broke apart momentarily.

Holly pulled off her tank and he stripped off his shirt. When he pulled her to him, they were skin against steamy skin. Her apartment wasn't very hot, but she and Nick created their own blazing heat. Warmth pooled in her belly, her sex, when Nick didn't return to kissing her mouth but instead kissed her exposed neck, nipping at her shoulder.

Holly slipped her hands into his back pockets, loving the feel of his perfectly muscled butt. Not removing her hands, she pulled Nick to her. The feel of his erection between them emboldened her to go further. She unbuckled his leather belt, unzipped him, and pulled his erection from his boxer briefs.

Seeing Nick hang his head and close his eyes in pleasure as she stroked him pushed her desire to a higher plane. They moved to her bedroom in a timeless waltz, removing more clothes, and devouring each others' mouths along the way.

By the time they reached her bedroom, Nick was completely nude, his erection straining to meet her. Only Holly's lacy, black bikini panties remained. When she bent to remove them, bracing herself on the bed, Nick held her back. "No, keep them on. They're incredibly sexy." Then he instructed her, "Bend over."

She did as she was told, resting on her forearms on her high mattress, her bottom, a feast for his eyes. Where she would have normally been unsettled having a man to stare at her more than generous assets, something about the rapidness of Nick's breathing reassured her that her ample derriere was an enormous turn-on for him.

Not seeing Nick or knowing what he was going to do next heightened her anticipation, her pleasure. She gasped when she felt his iron hard erection press against the crevice of her bottom. The gentle rasp of Nick moving against her caused her nipples to pucker. No sooner than her nipples hardened did Nick graze his hot palms against the tips of her breasts, now pendulous by virtue of her position.

The barest scrape of his calloused hands was exquisite torture. The sound of a tearing foil packet nearly set her teeth on edge. In a moment, she knew, Nick would fill her. She almost came when his fingers brushed against her sex to move her panties to the side, exposing her fully to him.

His cock teased her at first, gliding up and down her channel, her moisture causing the most delicious friction. Their cries of satisfaction were simultaneous when he plunged into her to the hilt. As he pulled almost free, then thrust, slowly at first, then faster as the tension built, the duvet's smooth cotton delicately chafing against her nipples was sweet torture.

When they were both close to the edge, she felt Nick's fingers parting her folds and caressing her clit, slowly, then harder and faster, as his thrusts increased tempo. At that moment, she looked up and realized she could see their reflections in her ornately carved floor mirror. She didn't watch erotic movies, but staring at Nick's aroused face, then her own, their bodies moving in rhythm, was as exciting as the most intimate touch. When her eyes met Nick's in the mirror, they came almost simultaneously, their cries mingling in the dark room.

Impasse

Holly felt bereft when Nick pulled out and went into her small master bathroom to clean himself. Feeling as strong as wet spaghetti, she collapsed on the bed, rolling on her back and staring wordlessly up to the ceiling. Nick came back into the room. Before Holly could speak, before she could launch into her routine "I'm really tired, you should get going" speech, Nick spoke.

"Holly, I don't think I can do this anymore."

Her heart skipped a few beats, and her stomach plummeted to her toes, but she kept up the bravest face she could muster. If Nick wanted to call it quits, that was his right. They didn't have any kind of hold on each other. A few weeks of great sex did not equal commitment. When she didn't respond, Nick grabbed her hand, pulling her up to a sitting position, and answered the question that had lodged itself in her throat like a lump of difficult-to-swallow vegetables. "I don't want to break up with you, I just… I want… Holly, I don't know why this is so hard between us. I want to spend the night with you."

She pulled back physically and emotionally. "Nick, that's not a good idea."

"Holly, I don't want to sleep with you," he said with a devilish grin when her expression turned incredulous, "not this minute anyway. I want to spend the night sleeping with you."

"What about the rules? You promised—"

"I know, but this is the only way I can do this right now."

Do what? She wanted to know. But dreading crossing the line into the prohibited "relationship zone," she didn't ask.

She tried not to let the trepidation she felt show on her face. "Sure, whatever, but you don't have a change of clothes," she said, her tone as blasé as she could make it. His words and actions were slowly chipping away at the granite that had formed around her heart after Drew.

"I have everything I need in my gym bag." Hmm, so Nick had anticipated this line of defense.

While Holly showered and changed back into her tank top and fresh undies, brushed her teeth, and tied her hair back into a ponytail for bed, Nick brushed his teeth and pulled on a pair of boxers. He filled the doorframe, muscular arms crossed, watching Holly. He admired her as she smoothed cream on her face and neck at her vanity. Holly organized her brush and comb on the carved wood surface of her vanity. She started straightening her cosmetics, then moved to cleaning out her drawers. Holly started when Nick spoke, his breath on her neck. She hadn't heard him walk toward her.

"Come to bed, Holly," he said, his tone insistent.

"Remember I have to get up early tomorrow—last minute volunteer arrangements and such. So you're not going to get that much of a good night's sleep here."

Ignoring her, he pulled back the duvet and she got in the bed, lying stiffly on one side. Nick climbed in next to her and pulled the covers over them both. "Come here," Nick said gruffly, pulling Holly into his arms. She went willingly this time, out of things to do, out of excuses to make, her head resting in the crook of his shoulder, her leg inserted between his.

"Holly, what are you afraid of? Tell me."

"This. Us," she said, dropping her voice.

"Why? I would never do anything to hurt you."

"I'm sure you never would, intentionally," Holly whispered.

"I just worry that if we get involved, really involved, you'll get bored and leave when the next young girl comes along."

"But I want to be with you, Holly. I don't have any plans to go anywhere or be with anyone else."

"For right now," she said, not able to hide her skepticism.

"What do I have to do to get you to trust me?"

"I don't have all the answers, Nick." Then she turned her face and spoke into his shoulder, worried he'd see emotions she couldn't hide. "I don't want to need you, Nick, or love you and have you leave me. It would kill me this time. I don't think my heart could take it… "

He didn't ask any more of her, just stroked her back until her breathing evened out and deepened.

Holly usually had trouble falling asleep. Often she would have warm milk, or play soothing music to relax. But that night in Nick's arms, she slept better than she had in years.

Nick's plan, hatched last night, was halfway done. One by one, he was getting past the rules. He'd managed to get past her defenses and convinced her to let him spend the night at her place. And what a night it had been. It was exactly like that first perfect night with her. Just Holly and him, no walls, no barriers, no pretense. No rules.

It wasn't that Nick didn't enjoy sleeping with—no, making love with—Holly, but spending time with her, getting to know her, getting beyond her defenses and protests put him one step closer to convincing her that they could go for the long haul.

Those thoughts pushed Nick to carefully untangle himself from Holly and pull himself out of bed no matter how comfortable he was. It was time to move on with step two of the plan. Careful not to wake her, Nick made his way to the living room to make a couple of quick calls on his cell phone.

When Holly finally stretched herself awake, Nick was sitting in her wing-back chair, freshly shaved, showered, and dressed, reading her copy of the weekend paper.

"Did you shower already?" she asked, looking at the clock and realizing it was much later than she should have slept in on a Saturday morning. "Oh, my God, you should have woken me up. I can't be late."

Nick shook his head. Folding the sports section into his lap, he made direct eye contact with her. "Hey, lazybones. Don't worry, I've got it all sorted out."

"What do you mean?" Holly asked, frantically pulling a pair of jeans and worn chambray shirt from her closet.

"While you slept in, I called the Dean of Students from Nueva Esperanza, and he's bringing over a few kids who are low on their volunteer hours. Sophie's already agreed to help, and my father will be there as well."

"Nick, I don't know what to say. This is such a relief." Holly buckled her watch, then looked at the time. "I still have to get going. I'm the coordinator, and I can't be late."

"I'll drive."

"You're coming, too?"

"I would never leave you in the lurch. I'd be honored to spend the day helping where I can."

There was only one car in the small parking lot when they arrived at the Korby Center. Nick pulled up alongside a sleek Acura.

Impasse

"Nick, Ryan volunteered to help us out today."

"Ryan?"

"From the restaurant… my, um, date," Holly said wrinkling her nose.

"It's all good," he said casually. "That Ryan and I," Nick gestured with his hand, "we've got a lot in common."

"What's that?" she asked, looking confused.

Nick leaned across the gearshift toward the passenger seat and gently grabbed Holly's chin, swiveling her face toward his. "We both know how special you are." He kissed her softly. It was a kiss not of passion, but something more, something deeper. "I understand that we have a lot to do today. Let's get to it."

Holly shouldn't have worried about having enough volunteers. While more Equia volunteers would have made the company look better, Dean Callas came through with a full contingent in tow. She'd already met Anthony and Carlos, who brought another four eager student volunteers in the school van. Sophie showed up with her now turquoise hair wrapped tightly in a bandana, in sturdy overalls, boots and gloves, ready to work.

Holly met briefly with the Korby Center residents, staff, and board members, and divided up the work. The kids from Nueva and Korby were assigned to the yard, first to clean up the debris and dead plants, then to transplant new flowers, shrubs, and trees. With Dominic's expertise to guide them, Holly thought it best that Nick, Sophie, Ryan, and she work on the inside—painting the bedrooms and the recreation room, and arranging the new furniture Equia had donated.

Holly hadn't spent a lot of time with Nick out of bed in the last few weeks. She had forgotten how funny and charming he could be. Even though they were working hard to finish the project in one day as she had promised, he kept everyone's spirits up.

He bantered with Dominic, sharing stories of project disasters in his dad's years as a contractor. Even Ryan got into it teasing Sophie. Looking at them, Holly thought she saw sparks. Now that would be an interesting turn of events. Ryan was as straight laced as one could get, and Sophie was adventurous to a fault.

Nick saw the obvious chemistry, too.

"Do you think they'd ever get together?" Nick whispered only partially in jest when Sophie and Ryan were out of earshot.

"I don't think so," Holly said, laughing and shaking her head.

"Why?" Nick asked, genuinely perplexed by her attitude.

"He's a lot more like me," Holly said matter-of-factly, "and Sophie's… well, Sophie."

"And what does that mean?"

"He strikes me as the kind of guy who wants to plant roots. Sophie's the kind of person who wants to grow wings."

With the work completed late in the afternoon, Holly and the others toured their progress. Holly was grateful that the board members and residents were happy with the job they'd done. As with other projects Holly had supervised, fewer volunteers were sometimes better. There were enough people to get the work done, but not so many that people were getting in each other's way.

Nick was looking around the center with the others, proud of the work they had done, when he came across a young looking girl sulking in a corner. He knelt down so he could see eye to eye with the brown-skinned girl.

"You're Jalicia, right?" Nick asked.

The girl only nodded, silent.

"It's been a real pleasure working on your house today. Are you happy with the way things turned out?"

She nodded again, tears gathering in her eyes.

"What's wrong?"

The girl wiped her eyes and nose unceremoniously. "You guys have been so nice. But you'll go to your nice houses in Beverly Hills or in West L.A., and we'll be here alone again."

"The people who run the center seem very nice and encouraging," Nick said, at a loss as to how to soothe this young woman.

"They are nice. And it was very special what they arranged for our rooms today. It's just that all this," she said with a sweeping gesture, "doesn't make my mom and dad okay so I can go home and live with them."

Nick sighed, and leaned back on his haunches. "I won't claim that I can relate to you. I grew up with both my parents and my sister and brother in a great home. My mom didn't work and took care of us kids. My dad did all he could to spend time with us and teach us how to be self-sufficient. I know that I was luckier than most kids. But I know plenty of people who've had it rougher who have found success and happiness in their lives," Nick said. "You know Holly, the woman who organized this event?"

The girl smiled. "Your girlfriend?"

Nick grinned. "I'm working on that. Anyway, she's one amazing lady. She almost single-handedly pulled all this together.

She's confident, smart, and beautiful. However, more than that, she's an orphan. Her parents died when she was young, but she made the best of things and look at where she is now."

The girl glanced up as Holly walked into the room.

Nick continued. "She's an incredible woman as I'm sure you will be one day. Jalicia Howard, right?" Nick said. "I just hope you still remember me when you're wealthy and successful."

The girl walked out of the room, her head higher, and her gait more confident than before. Moved by what she had just witnessed, Holly pulled Nick outside to a shaded and secluded area on the side of the building. "Nick, I just want to thank you. I'm sure you probably would like to have spent your weekend doing something more fun—" Holly didn't get a chance to finish her thought before Nick broke in.

"My perfect day, Holly, is any day I spend with you, no matter what we're doing. I can't imagine anywhere I'd rather be."

Holly felt her stomach quiver with nerves and a lump form in her throat. These were all the right words she'd waited her life to hear—but they were coming from the wrong person. Theirs was a no commitment, no frills relationship. She broke his unwavering gaze when, gratefully, she heard one of the Korby people calling her name. It was time to finish up here and get home.

There were hugs and tears all around. A number of the young women in the shelter wept silently. They had said several times that in all their years of foster care, they'd never had people take the time to put together rooms of their own. It had been a surprise when one of the board members had presented each girl with a hand-embroidered pillow for her room in a favorite color, with her name stitched in.

Nick drove them. Holly was quiet, overcome with a whole gamut of emotions she couldn't put a name to. She usually didn't participate directly in the volunteer activities. Holly would never be able to get all of her other work done if that were the case, but occasionally she jumped into these "done in a day" projects. It helped her remember why she loved her job, especially on those interminable mornings filled with endless budget and marketing meetings. It was on days like today that she was never so happy that she had changed the direction of her career. Holly could see that she was making a real impact on the community.

He pulled into a parking space near her building and followed her up to her apartment without invitation, like they were a real couple.

"Are you hungry? I could throw together a little something for dinner."

"Do you mind?" he asked wearily.

"No, you did a lot of the heavy lifting today. Go. Relax in the living room. I'll need about twenty minutes."

Holly found only some late summer squash and a wedge of parmesan cheese in the fridge. She pulled out pasta, an egg, and some garlic and got to work. She heard the TV come on and knew Nick had gotten comfortable. Twenty minutes later, she had a hearty zucchini carbonara ready to serve.

"Nick?"

He didn't answer. Holly stepped into the living room only to see that he had dozed off on the couch. Forgetting dinner for a moment, Holly gazed at him. His perfect features were beautiful when he slept. She walked over and gingerly sat down next to him on the sofa. Holly caressed his chiseled features lightly, and when he didn't stir, she continued her exploration, greedily taking him in. She touched his dark, gently waving hair that, like hers, sometimes seemed to have a life of its own. She smoothed her hand along his jaw, rough with half a day's stubble. When she rubbed a thumb along his full masculine lower lip, Nick grasped her wrist, startling her. Her first reaction was to snatch her hand away, but he held her firm.

"Dinner's ready," Holly said unnecessarily. The odor of garlic, olive oil, and sautéed vegetables had permeated the small apartment.

Nick pulled Holly to him, and suddenly off kilter, she landed solidly on his chest. Nick gave her another of those sweet, gentle kisses filled with more promise than sensuality.

They ate in the kitchen. The light from the range hood, the only illumination in the room, created an oddly romantic atmosphere. They relived much of the day, reigniting the joy they had felt at giving back. He told her that Dean Callas had described the experience as transforming for the Esperanza Nueva kids. They hadn't realized that while they didn't have it so great, at least they had parents and families around.

"How old is that couch I fell asleep on?"

"The Edwardian settee you mean?" Holly clarified. "It was handed down to my grandmother. From the early 1900s. Like most of the furniture here and in storage, my grandparents passed it down. It holds a lot of memories, some good, and some bad—but all important, I guess."

"Tell me one of the good ones."

Holly's eyes became unfocused as she turned inward, reliving old memories. "Nana used to tell me how Gramps proposed to her on that settee. She was living in the outskirts of London during the war and met Gramps there while volunteering to help the Allied servicemen. They dated for a while, and when the Allies declared victory, he came to my great-grandparents' house. I think the house had suffered in the bombing, but some of the living areas were spared.

"Anyway, Nana always tells how my Gramps, young and shy, and unapologetically American came into this really conservative British household and asked for her hand in marriage. She was sitting on that exact couch, as you call it, and he knelt down on one knee and asked her to marry him. When she came to America as a war bride, she felt very alone and disconnected from the place she grew up, so her parents shipped this over to help with her homesickness."

After they companionably cleaned the kitchen and loaded the dishwasher, Holly felt the same familiar awkwardness that plagued her whenever Nick was getting too close. But she wanted to be with him, rules be damned. "Do you want to stay over tonight?" she asked in what she hope sounded offhand.

If she were looking at Nick instead of looking down, Holly would have seen the look of relief and a little bit of triumph in his eyes.

When they were nestled under the covers, Holly comfortably lying in his arms, he quietly whispered another question. "What's the worst memory you have on that settee of yours?"

She sighed. "I think it was the time I realized that my parents weren't coming back. When they first disappeared, I was young and didn't quite understand what had happened. Little kids don't understand death. Later, though, I was mad at my grandparents for some stupid reason that I don't even remember. I told them I was packing my bags and going home. They explained it the same way they always had, but I got it that day that my parents were dead and never, ever coming back. I remember crying for a very long time, tracing the gold thread that wove its way through the cushions."

Nick felt warm damp tears streak down his shoulder, and he pulled her tighter to him, sorry he had made her cry.

In the dim light of the room, he watched Holly's eyes flutter closed, her breathing deepen. He had tried to express what he really wanted to say to her the last couple of days without saying it directly, instead by doing everything he could to make Holly's life easier. When he was sure she was asleep, he lay back, shielding his eyes from the streetlight that lit up slivers of her bedroom, and spoke from his heart. "Holly, despite your rules, I'm falling in love with you." Nick whispered, knowing he was the only one who heard. "You mean more to me than you know. I want to make beautiful memories for you, for us."

For the first time in the two months they'd been "together," they slept together without making love. He couldn't remember when just sleeping with a woman had been so satisfying.

"I never stay in bed this late, especially two days in a row," Holly said stretching, then yawning lazily.

"Hey, sleepyhead, don't fret. I'm in no hurry. You're the only person on my agenda today."

"Do you… I mean, I could make you breakfast or something

if you want before I get to my usual list of errands."

"I love your cooking, but I'm not asking you to do that this morning. Is there anything you have to do that can't wait?"

"No," she said. Sure, she needed to tackle the shopping, cleaning, and other stuff that she hadn't yet done that weekend, but suddenly seemed less interesting than what Nick had in mind. "Not really."

"Then let me surprise you," Nick said. "Why don't you get dressed?"

Holly quickly put herself together, trying to ignore Nick's seeming comfort with her morning routine. Given the vagaries of Los Angeles weather, she layered her clothing. They could end up anywhere from the mountains to the beach, which were both blustery and cold this time of year. On the other hand, if Nick drove for an hour, they could be in the desert with its relentless sun. She donned a sleeveless turtleneck, a Fair Isle patterned wool and angora sweater, and took along a jacket for good measure. Despite the cool and foggy morning, Nick put the top down and they cruised along the Santa Monica freeway, which was for once mercifully free of traffic.

When they emerged from the freeway tunnel and transitioned onto the Pacific Coast Highway, Holly took in the awesome sight of the Pacific Ocean. No matter how long she lived in Los Angeles, she never tired of the sea. This late in the morning, they passed wet-suited surfers coming in from hitting the waves, walking their boards across the PCH, as locals called it, toward the beach restaurants for a late brunch.

It was fun being in beautiful, natural surroundings, the convertible following the contours of the land, the Santa Monica

Mountains jutting up on the right; the coastline, jagged and rocky in some places, sandy in others, flanking their left. They passed the quaint center of the Pacific Palisades and came to the shores of Malibu.

Nick pulled off the highway on to a winding road that spiraled to the top of a hill. At the restaurant's entrance, they left the Mercedes with a valet, and stepped on to the quaintest patio Holly had ever seen. The hostess greeted them warmly, and Nick mentioned their eleven o'clock reservation. He had made a reservation. Holly thought Nick flew by the seat of his pants. They'd never really had plans. He usually called only half an hour before they got together. When had he arranged all of this?

They were led to a patio table, which overlooked the Malibu cliffs. Star jasmine wove through the patio's trellis frame, giving the patio a light but pleasant vanilla-like fragrance. Though it was a chilly morning, high above the water, the patio was flanked with outdoor gas heaters going at full blast, which made Holly feel downright cozy.

Conversation came surprisingly easily. Thankfully, they were back in the rhythm of old friends. Holly learned more about Nick's documentaries. He was finishing up the editing on the film about the kids and Esperanza Nueva, and his partner Helena was preparing entries for the film festivals that would be juried early next year.

For just an instant, a twinge of jealousy twisted her gut. Nick spoke so fondly of Helena. But Holly quickly shook it off. It was only appropriate that Nick speak of his partner and friend with warmth. There wasn't exactly an appropriate term of endearment for your three-times-a week booty call. Every last person had a place in Nick's life, Helena, his other colleagues, his dad. Holly, his sex partner didn't, and it was her own doing. It shouldn't have rubbed her the wrong way, but it did.

Their waitress appeared, and Holly ordered a pot of English tea and the ricotta cheese and seasonal berry pancakes. Nick chose Eggs Benedict served on homemade corn tortillas. Her meal was absolutely delicious, but Holly still eyed Nick's breakfast covetously, thinking maybe she should have ordered eggs instead. Finally, Nick paused about halfway through his plate.

"You want to switch breakfasts?"

Holly had been caught. "No. Okay… yes. Do you mind? It just looks so good."

"No, I don't mind," he said shaking his head ruefully. "This way we both get to try different things."

Holly was warmed by his generosity. Drew hadn't believed in sharing. On more than one occasion, he'd batted her hand away when she'd tried to sneak a morsel from his plate. Eventually, the waitress came to clear their plates. Holly poured and savored the last of her sweet milky tea, while Nick finished his mineral water. She watched the strong column of his throat and his Adam's apple bob as he swallowed. An answering achiness caused her to shift, cross her legs in response.

What was wrong with her? When did the simple act of watching this man drink water bring her to the knife-edge of desire? Nick placed his empty glass on the table and watched her watch him.

His smile, though, was enigmatic. Nick leaned forward, his hand grazing Holly's cheek. He carefully tucked her hair behind her ears so her whole face was exposed to his view. "Holly, I need to say a few things." Before she could shake her head in protest, he continued. "Just listen, please. I want you to think about what I'm saying, what I'm going to ask you, but I don't want you to answer me today." Nick's eyes fastened on hers as he exhaled—as if he were gathering his strength, his resolve.

"Holly, I love your hair, your smile, your spirit," he began. "I know you're not looking for a relationship with me at this stage in your life. But I enjoy having a good time with you, and I want more. I want to be fully committed to you." Nick paused and shook his head. "I don't want to beat around the bush here. I love you, Holly. I've wanted to say that every time I see you, every time we make love, but I've been trying to honor your wishes. I'm not just here for the short term. I want to marry you, someday."

Holly's stomach bottomed out. To save the last bit of sanity she had left, she tried to completely ignore what he'd just said. She started to interrupt him, to stop him from saying anything further, but before she could utter a word, he placed a finger to her lips. She immediately felt that same thrill of desire she now associated with Nick, but there was another feeling there as well, lurking under the surface—a feeling she wasn't quite ready to acknowledge or return.

"Nick, I'm not ready for this. This is why I wanted certain rules. We should not be having this conversation," Holly said, pleading with her eyes for more space, more time to figure out what was going on between them before putting a name to it.

"I don't need you to answer me now. Just think about what I said. I know there could be an 'us' if you'll just let it happen." His fingers cupped her head tilting her face toward his. "Helena and I are going to New York this week to meet with some cable

Impasse

network folks for a new documentary we're trying to get funding for. Think about what I said while I'm gone. If it's easier for you, I won't call you—that way you can decide whether you want there to be an 'us' with no pressure from me."

Nick hoped his face didn't reveal his longing for her to say yes to him, to them. This was the first time in his life that he really wanted something—someone—but was almost powerless to make it happen. He nearly ached with his need to possess her.

He leaned back, working at making his face neutral, and the mood changed. After flagging down their waitress, he settled the bill. When he turned back to her, he made sure his face was light, as if erasing the previous conversation. "No more heavy talk. I promised you a fun, frolicking day, so let's get to it."

The day had warmed considerably as they drove south on the PCH. Holly didn't need her jacket but was happy to have the sweater to keep the wind from raising goose bumps on her arms. At first, Holly didn't recognize the turn-off they made into Santa Monica. They parked behind a series of interconnected buildings that looked like an old train depot.

"Are we at Bergamot Station?" she asked, suddenly recalling articles she'd read about the area's renaissance. The reclaimed train depot housed the Santa Monica Museum of Art and a few other galleries of local artists. "I've always wanted to come here."

Nick nodded. "You mentioned it a few years ago during a dinner at your house. I think you'll like the current exhibition."

She gasped then coughed to hide her reaction. He remembered that? Nick had remembered that little detail from small talk at a party? She pulled her trembling fist from where it covered her mouth and laid it against her stomach, hoping for calm. His feelings might be real. How could she have failed to see that this 'relationship' or whatever it was—meant that much to Nick? And he was right, she loved the museum. The exhibition was a selection of paintings by lesser known English and American artists from the early twentieth century. It was the kind of art her grandparents had collected and passed down to her.

For more than an hour, as she wandered among the artists' works, Holly tried to work out what would happen next with Nick. Determined to put the hard questions off for a time, she wandered among the art. Some of it was achingly familiar, others canvases were new, but similar in style to the paintings that had surrounded her when she was growing up. Nick asked a few questions about the artists and the paintings but was generally quiet, respectful of her contemplation.

After leaving the exhibit, they wandered among the many galleries sharing the space at the station. At one point, Holly considered buying a painting but decided against the indulgence. Her apartment barely had enough space for her grandmother's things, much less additional furniture or art.

Nick's exuberance was infectious. He was having a good time and by extension so was Holly. When they had toured a number of galleries and had their fill of art, Holly couldn't wait to see what Nick had planned for the rest of the day.

"So what's next?" she asked, expectantly.

Nick smiled mischievously. "Holly, and I say this only in the kindest way, I think we need to loosen you up. Age is a state of mind. You're still young. So I thought we'd do something you'd never do on your own."

Holly quelled her slight trepidation. His enthusiasm was infectious. "Okay, I'm game."

"I was hoping you'd say that." Once in Nick's convertible, they made the short drive west on Pico Boulevard to one of the public parking lots on the beach. They walked on The Strand, the small pedestrian walkway that followed the contours of the Pacific's coastline. To the right of them cyclists, runners, and in-line skaters enjoyed the sun and sand. Nick clasped her hand as they walked, and for once Holly didn't pull away. It felt good. She was going to let herself feel good with Nick. She couldn't promise that she'd agree to the relationship he asked for, but that didn't mean she couldn't enjoy him like he was a real boyfriend, instead of just her boy-toy lover.

While they walked along the beach, she looked back and forth at the street vendors' wares . Some were selling art, others jewelry, still others appeared to be selling nothing more than a hope for world peace. There were also the ubiquitous, hugely built guys working out at Muscle Beach. The throng of people wove a tapestry that was uniquely Venice Beach. When Nick led Holly to a woman displaying beautifully intricate tattoo designs, Holly looked at Nick hesitantly. "Nick, I don't think I'm drunk enough for this."

Nick laughed out loud at her quip. "Don't worry, they're not permanent. They're henna tattoos. No beer necessary."

The young Indian woman who ran the stand sized them up as likely buyers.

"Hi, I'm Mala," she said grasping their hands in both of hers.

"Are you thinking of getting some henna art?"

Holly shook her head while Nick nodded. Mala laughed. "Don't worry, they wash off in three to four weeks. I think something like this," she said gesturing to a few intricate designs, "would look beautiful on your skin." Mala looked slyly at Nick. "Plus, I think your boyfriend would really like it." Holly started to correct her but changed her mind when she saw the happy look on Nick's face.

She was going to do it. Why the heck not? Even Sophie had a tattoo, though hers was permanent. Holly had always secretly admired the young girls who tattooed the small of their backs and wore low rise jeans to show them off.

Though Holly knew she wasn't the kind to permanently alter her body, she was intrigued by the idea of having a sexy temporary tattoo that only she and Nick knew about. After looking at the designs the artist displayed, Holly decided to have a labyrinthine flower design applied to the small of her back. After changing out of her jeans behind a makeshift screen, Holly laid face down on the massage chair and let the tattoo artist do her work. Since Mala said it would take about fifteen minutes, Nick volunteered to get them some water. Mala kept up a patter the entire time she deftly flicked the tiny natural bristle brush along Holly's back.

"Your boyfriend's real cute. He seems nice, too."

"He's not my boyfriend. We're just… " Holly trailed off, uncertain how to finish her thought.

"If he isn't your boyfriend, you should snap him up before someone else does. He doesn't seem like the kind of guy to be alone for long."

When Mala was done, Holly changed back into her street

clothes and opened her purse to pay.

Mala motioned for her to put away her wallet. "Your 'non-boyfriend' already paid and gave me a nice tip. Just follow the directions on this sheet, and be sure to keep that hunky guy warm at night." Mala winked as she handed Holly instructions on maintaining her temporary tattoo. Nick chose that moment to join them. The women broke into simultaneous laughter.

"It's nothing," Holly said, opening the plastic bottle and taking a swig of the cold water Nick had brought. "Onward to the next adventure."

"Now the fun begins," Nick said. "Let's stop at the grocery store, then go home."

When they pulled up to Ralph's, further east on Pico Boulevard, Holly's curiosity got the best of her. "What are we getting?"

"You'll see. C'mon." Nick grabbed her hand and they trotted to the automatic doors. He grabbed a basket and headed toward the back of the store. "I tell you what. You pick a beer for us to drink, and I'll get the food." Holly wandered over to the refrigerator aisle and considered the hundreds of beers on offer. She remembered having some good Belgian beers some years before in Europe, and she picked up a six-pack of sour cherry infused lambic she found on the shelves. Nick was already in line when she reached him. His basket was full of chips, fresh tomatoes, avocados, Mexican chilies, as well as refried beans, ground meat, and a couple of different cheeses.

"I presume we're having nachos."

"You presume correctly," he said, making fun of her sometimes formal speech. He planted a quick kiss on the top of her head. "Fun food for a fun day."

For a few minutes when they pulled up to Nick's house and brought the groceries to the kitchen, Holly basked in the fantasy that they were a real couple. They got along well. And the more time she spent at his house, the more at home she felt. To top it off, she didn't think it would take much for her to fall in love with him, and that scared her more than anything else in the world.

They worked companionably in the kitchen. Holly made fresh salsa and guacamole. Nick fried up the beef and laid the tortilla chips on a large baking sheet. He then piled them high with toppings and popped them in the oven. Holly had to smile. For all his so-called maturity, he had moments where he acted like a big kid. She could accuse him of having eyes bigger than his stomach but refrained, lest he think she was trying out for the part of grandma. While the nachos baked, Nick set up the living room. He pulled out the large throw pillows and plugged a console game into the large screen television.

"Wait," Holly said. "We're playing video games? I don't normally do this kind of stuff. I don't have the dexterity for those tiny controls nor the stomach for gory shoot 'em up games."

Nick ignored her and continued plugging in wires while she pulled the bubbling, cheesy nachos from the oven and piled their plates high. "It's not that kind of game," he finally said. "I don't have the stomach for those violent ones either. It'll be fun. Trust me."

Holly doubted him, but went along anyway. She'd enjoyed the day more than she'd anticipated. Nick was a lot of fun, and maybe, just maybe, age was a state of mind.

While she ate gooey nachos with her fingers and sipped at

the cool beer, Nick loaded up a Tomb Raider adventure game. Holly didn't expect much from the scantily clad, gun-toting heroine, Lara Croft. But the game was surprisingly enjoyable. There was adventure, spectacular graphics, and problem solving. Nick and Holly spent as much time manipulating the controls as they did with pen and paper working out the numerous puzzles and riddles the game presented.

Holly couldn't remember having such a good time just playing around. She felt more lighthearted than she had in years. Before she knew it, they had finished most of the nachos. When she looked at her watch to check the time, she was surprised to discover it was already nine-thirty. While Nick was consulting the game guide for clues to their current dilemma, Holly pressed the pause button on the console to mute the background sounds in the game.

It had been a great day and an incredible weekend. She got up and moved the remnants of their meal into the kitchen and loaded the dishwasher. When she returned to the living room, she pulled the strategy guide from Nick's hands. She wanted to make him feel as good as he had made her feel. He was sitting on the floor, long legs fully extended, so she scooted her bottom between his legs, straddled her legs over his hips, looped her arms around his neck, and kissed him full on the mouth. In the back of her mind, she heard a thud as the controller hit the floor.

He broke the kiss, hesitantly, after some minutes. "Holly, we don't have to do anything," he said, his voice already slightly rough with arousal. "When I said I wanted to spend the day with you, I wasn't planning on making love to you. I wanted to explore the other parts of our relationship…" Nick trailed off as Holly stroked the hard musculature of his back, deliberately lingering in his most erogenous areas.

She looked at him from under her lashes. "Nick, I just want to explore your other parts." She could feel his breath in her hair as she unbuttoned his jeans. She was surprised that he was hard for her after only one kiss. She brushed the back of her hand along his erection, and he sucked in a breath.

"Holly…" Nick's feeble protest came to a grinding halt as she shifted her position, kneeling between his legs. She leaned into him, and her breath caressed his boxer briefs. She lifted his penis from his shorts and rubbed at the beaded moisture on the tip with the soft pad of her thumb. Nick's only response was a deep groan. There was no resistance when she moved away to strip off his pants and underwear and position herself more firmly between his thighs. She pressed her breasts against his balls and grasped his cock firmly in her hands. She then took him as deep as she could in her mouth, sucking and licking her way to the tip, again, and again, and again, Nick writhing beneath her. A groan hissed from Nick's lips as she pleasured him in earnest.

"Oh, God, Holly, I'm going to come," Nick said through clenched teeth.

Holly didn't stop and was rewarded with Nick's orgasm, which seemed to go on forever, his organ jerking of its own volition.

"You didn't have to do that."

"I wanted to," Holly said meaning it, swallowing his essence.

"Let's go to bed."

They left the mess for the ants, walking, fingers entwined, upstairs to his bedroom. She undressed, unselfconsciously for once, and pulled back the covers in the huge sleigh bed, illuminated only by moonlight. Holly didn't know when, but she'd made up her mind about Nick that day. Why shouldn't she give it a try? What did she have to lose being with Nick? Holly didn't probe the answer to that rhetorical question too deeply because she suspected that what she could lose was her heart.

When Nick turned on the light, revealing the now wine-colored bedroom, Holly was taken aback. "Nick, when did you paint this? It makes me feel right at home." To demonstrate, Holly launched herself at the bed and rolled around gleefully.

He undressed silently, and they slid under the covers. Nick reached up to turn out the one lamp, and the room was again bathed in the moon's ethereal glow.

"I guess you still don't have those curtains."

"No, but this way I can see all of you," Nick whispered huskily. He gently tugged at her hair, watching the spirals bounce back from his touch. "Holly," he started, looking directly into her eyes, "I love your hair. It's wild and crazy. I love that it tells me that you're more than the conservative, down-to-earth person you project." Nick continued caressing her, his hands whispering along her smooth back. "I love your back. It's smooth and yet firm, showing that you have the courage of your convictions." His touch tickled the small of her back. "I love knowing that you have this tattoo, for my eyes only." He caressed the moons of her bottom. "I love your ass. It's so feminine, and it really turns me on."

With only his hands, Nick gently urged Holly to turn over. She was lying on her back now, staring at the ceiling, her eyes avoiding the intensity of his scrutiny. When his fingers traced her areola, glanced off her nipple, Holly shuddered involuntarily. "I love your breasts." When she shook her head, almost imperceptibly, and brought her hands reflexively over them out of habit, Nick pulled her hands away. "Holly, you shouldn't be embarrassed about the size of your breasts. If any man ever told you that you weren't attractive—" Nick bit off the rest of the sentence. His tones returned to soothing ones.

"A handful is more than enough for me. What turns me on more than any one body part itself is your responsiveness. I love knowing that I can tweak you here," he tweaked her nipple, "or lick you there," he played on her other nipple with the point of his tongue, "and know that you respond so willingly." Involuntarily, Holly shuddered.

Nick traced her collarbone, skimmed his palms along her toned thighs, complimented her shapely calves, worshipped the rest of her nude form. Holly's limbs felt languorous. She wanted to touch him, to tell him how cherished she felt, but she was unable to speak, suddenly tired, and instead was lulled into a deep peaceful sleep. The sleep of someone whose decision to break the rules had lifted a huge weight from her shoulders.

Holly woke to the smell of breakfast. Just when she had propped herself up on the unmistakably new and plump pillows, Nick came in with heaping plates on a wooden tray. Shirtless in loose-fitting sweats, he looked more delectable than breakfast. But out of politeness, she made an effort to look interested in the food.

Wordlessly, he slid the tray over her legs. He had made scrambled eggs, bacon, whole wheat English muffins, orange

Impasse

juice, and of course, English tea. They didn't talk about anything in particular while they ate. Holly was about to thank him when she felt overcome with an acute sense of nausea. She was just able to set the tray aside, and make it to the bathroom, before she lost her breakfast.

Nick rushed in behind her, holding back her hair while her stomach contents emptied.

"Maybe I should leave the cooking up to you," Nick chided.

"I'm so mortified," Holly said, her face coloring deeply. "I don't know what happened."

Nick got a washcloth and gently wiped her forehead, mouth, and neck. He rummaged in the bathroom drawers and gave her a new toothbrush. While she was brushing her teeth, a towel tucked modestly around her breasts, Nick brought her a soft old college t-shirt from his University of Illinois days and a pair of his old boxers. She put them on. The t-shirt draped to her knees, but was supremely comfortable and smelled of Nick—a far better smell than breakfast, or what had come after. Thankfully, the bedroom was devoid of food when she got back into bed.

"Nick," she called out. She thought she heard a muffled yes from the kitchen over the sound of the garbage disposal devouring the remainder of her breakfast. "I don't feel so well, do you mind if I take a little nap before I go home?"

She picked up her cell phone and called in sick to work, then closed her eyes for a quick nap.

Holly was out cold. Nick watched her sleep soundly and did his best not to wake her. He pulled out his luggage from the loft's small storage area and packed his clothes as quietly as he could. When Nick came back down to the bedroom to get more clothes out of the armoire, Holly was just coming awake.

"How are you feeling?"

"I'm fine," Holly said.

To Nick, she looked really tired, off' somehow.

"Can you drop me off at home?" she asked. "If time is tight with your flight and all, I can get a ride from—"

Nick cut her off. "Of course I can drive you home. It's on the way to Helena's house anyway." He paused, looking at her again. "Are you sure you're okay?"

Holly and Nick talked about everything but their "relationship" on the short drive to her house. When he pulled the convertible to a stop, Holly looked at her watch. "You don't have to walk me in. I'm fine Nick, just fine."

"I want to see for myself. Make sure you have what you need."

Holly did everything she could to keep up a perky persona. She didn't want the fact that she was dog-tired with the flu or some bug to keep Nick in L.A. His job, his projects were far too important for that.

"I'll be okay, Nick. I have plenty of good stuff like oatmeal, mac and cheese, and tea, lots of tea. Don't worry about me."

Nick leaned close to her, brushed her hair away from her face, and kissed her forehead, then her lips with the utmost tenderness. "Be well."

Holly trailed Nick as he let himself out. "Get well, I don't want anything to happen to my love," he said. Holly shut the door but didn't have the time to analyze his comment before a new wave of nausea hit her. But this time, her stomach was empty, so

Impasse

Holly got herself a glass of water and got into bed fully clothed. She'd get up later, after a little nap.

When her eyelids fluttered open for the third time that day, it was already dark outside. Damn, Holly thought, she'd slept the day away. She was starving now. Splurging on the calories, she made herself a large bowl of macaroni and cheese. She curled up in front of the TV with her favorite Hugh Grant movie in the DVD player.

Full and warm, Holly felt much better. It must have been a twelve-hour bug, she thought. She took a warm bath and tucked herself in bed later that night, feeling just fine.

It was another story on Tuesday morning. She woke up feeling great. She did a few yoga stretches, then got into the shower and dressed. But it all went wrong again at breakfast. Two bites of an English muffin and a few sips of tea had Holly back in the bathroom. She called in sick, again. Maybe it was more of a twenty-four to thirty-six hour bug. The folks at Equia could live without her for another day. She hadn't taken a sick day in more than five years.

Halfway through her second Hugh Grant movie, a holiday one this time, the phone rang.

"Hey, Sophie," Holly said, hearing enough background traffic noise to let her know that Sophie was outside somewhere on her cell.

"I stopped by your office to see if you were free for lunch. Your assistant told me you'd called in sick for the last two days. You okay?"

"Soph, I don't know. I got sick at Nick's place. I feel like I must have some kind of weird flu or something."

"I'm coming over."

"You don't have to do that. I thought you were on the set of one of the kid shows today."

"I have a couple of days free. The young star has to make up some missed school hours, so the crew's off."

Sophie asked some questions about Holly's condition, then said she'd stop by the store and be over in an hour. True to her word, Sophie was knocking on the door about the time Holly had finished her movie. Large drugstore sack in hand, Sophie bustled her way into the kitchen. She took out Pepto-Bismol, saltines, ginger ale, club soda, and a pregnancy test.

"Sophie, you're a godsend," Holly said, twisting the cap off the ginger ale and pouring herself a glass. "Wait, why did you buy that?" she said when she saw the test kit on the table. "I'm sick with some weird stomach flu, not pregnant."

Raising one pierced eyebrow skeptically, Sophie looked hard at Holly. "Clearly, I'm no medical expert, but you're acting a lot like my sister Selie did in her first trimester. When was your last period anyway?"

"I don't remember, but Nick and I have always used protection," she said emphatically. Then she paused. "Except—"

"Except for when?"

"Just that first time," Holly said, abashed. "We got a little carried away."

"Sounds like a lot carried away." Sophie pushed the slim pastel pink and blue box into Holly's hands. "Just do this to be sure. Then I'll take you to Canter's, and we can try the chicken soup cure."

Holly got up to go to the bathroom. Nick's voluminous shirt, which she was still wearing, rode up on her back.

"Girl, is that a tattoo I see? Nick's had some influence on you. Next thing you know, you'll be wearing skinny jeans."

Holly grimaced before pulling the t-shirt back down to her knees. "It's just a henna tattoo. Nick and I were on The Strand in Venice."

"No need to explain to me. I'm sure he thinks it's sexy," Sophie said with a wink. "Get in there. I'll put the kettle on for more tea."

Five long minutes stretched taut with silence. The kitchen timer buzzed at the same time the kettle whistled. Sophie poured hot water into Holly's Chinese tea pot, arranging two small mugs on a hand carved tray. Holly stepped toward the bathroom trepidation in every step. Two pink lines, one faint, one dark filled the tiny plastic window. Her steps back to the kitchen were as rapid as she could make them without breaking into a sprint. Hands shaking, heart palpitating, she nearly tripped over her feet thrusting the little telltale stick toward her friend.

Sophie paused, kettle in hand. "I guess one time was a charm."

Speechless, Holly nodded.

"Are you going to call Nick? I think he should be here with you, now. New York can wait." Sophie moved as if to get the cordless phone from its base on the wall.

"No, I don't want to tell him. Not now at least."

"Why not?"

"Sophie, he's twenty-six. He's not ready for fatherhood. I can't go through this whole thing again with Nick."

"What whole thing?" Sophie asked, clearly confused. Her best friend didn't know the half of it.

Holly got quiet, memories assailing her now. "When Drew

and I first got married, a few months before you and I met, I got pregnant."

Sophie gasped, a quick intake of breath. "I didn't know, hon."

"I've never told anyone. Drew didn't want the baby. He said we were too young, we hadn't been married long enough. He had a litany of excuses."

"What happened?"

"We fought, we argued. I was extremely stressed out. Happy one day, crying the next." She paused. Holly pushed out the four hardest words she'd said in a long time. "I lost the baby." There was another lull as she caught her breath and continued. "At the time it seemed like it was all for the best. We never tried again. That's why I don't want to put any of this on Nick. Sophie, he still doesn't have a couch, and his car only has two seats. Where would a car safety seat go?" Holly paused, momentarily quiet and contemplative.

"I really want this baby. I'd always planned for a baby, a family, for a very long time. No matter what Nick decides, I will raise our child. But, I won't cut his single, carefree life short. Please let me decide when to tell him; if…"

Her best friend shook her head, her disagreement obvious. "You should call that man right now. Let him make the decision. He may be a little younger than us, but he's a grown ass man who can handle the consequences of his actions," Sophie said, her customary gum cracking sarcasm gone for once. "You didn't make this baby alone. I may not have finished college, but I was a whiz at high school biology. It takes two."

"I don't know, Sophie. It's all too much," Holly said, tears welling up in her eyes. "Let me see if I can get into the doctor's

Impasse

office to confirm, and we'll go from there. All this hand wringing may be for nothing. How reliable can these home tests be anyway?"

Eight

Nick looked at his watch for the fifth time in as many minutes. It was only an hour into his six-hour cross-country flight and he was already restless. He was mentally cursing himself for leaving L.A. without finding out what Holly felt for him, and whether she was ready to make some kind of commitment beyond inundating their relationship with rules. Not knowing where they stood was wrecking his ability to concentrate on the tasks that lay ahead.

He fidgeted again, taking the cell phone from his pocket. Per airline regulations, the device was switched off. There would be no "message waiting" light beckoning him at thirty-five thousand feet. But, looking at the blank LCD screen, he still wondered if she'd left him a voice mail, maybe sent him a text message. Nick normally didn't take no for an answer. He couldn't say why he'd let Holly off the hook so easily.

The woman next to him paused her in-flight movie with

Impasse

the remote control and looked him directly in the eye. "Nick," Helena said. "It's going to be a really, really long flight if you don't stop squirming around so much. Why are you so restless? You're usually a pretty good flyer."

Nick looked at Helena, his closest friend and business partner for the past two years, and remained quiet. Their close working relationship meant very often no words were necessary for Nick to get his point across. When they were filming, much of their communication was non-verbal. She could read him across a room, much less across an arm rest.

"Ah, it must be a woman," she said knowingly, a sparkle in her eye. "I wondered when you'd finally succumb. Are you over Drew's ex-wife? Found someone who's—mmm—available?"

The intense glare he shot her, subdued Helena. "I see I've just stuck my pudgy little foot in it. So, bringing Holly to the Esperanza Nueva graduation wasn't some bid to raise money from Equia, was it? It was an honest-to-goodness bona fide date. I should have known something was going when you guys rushed out like that without even saying goodbye.

"Nick, don't get me wrong, I like Holly well enough. She's a really nice person, but are you doing the smart thing here?"

"Helena… " Nick warned.

"What? Don't look at me like that. I'm genuinely happy for you," Helena said, a hint of exasperation in her voice. "It's just that we've known Drew for years. He mentored you when we were both at the network. I mean, he's the one responsible, at least partially, for these meetings this week. Solstice is still a fledgling company, and we've been lucky so far. I don't want to lose that momentum. This is my business and career, too, you know."

He looked at her hard, but she continued anyway.

"All I'm asking is, are you sure she's not on the rebound? Our relationship with Drew is valuable to our careers, especially in a town like Los Angeles where 'who you know' is everything. He's our best contact. Not to mention his help with financing the post production on the Esperanza film."

"Don't you think I've thought of all that, Helena?" Nick exploded. "I'm not sure of anything at all, except I'm in love with her."

They both fell silent after Nick's proclamation, the thrum of the jet engine roaring in the background.

After a long moment, Helena asked in a quiet voice, "Are the feelings mutual?" Clearly she still adhered to her rebound theory.

"I don't know, but I really hope so."

Holly tried flipping through the news magazines piled high on her doctor's waiting room coffee table, but she couldn't concentrate. She couldn't wrap her head around the idea that she could really be pregnant. The latest tax cut policy detailed in the magazine on her lap paled in comparison to her amazement that a small life could possibly be growing inside her.

She'd wanted a baby for so long, and it could finally be happening. The circumstances weren't perfect. Far from it, she knew. She'd wanted to be married, maybe have a house, and at least be settled. Her doting husband would be by her side to share this momentous occasion. Instead she was carrying the baby of her sometime booty call, maybe boyfriend who wasn't by her side at all but in New York City, oblivious to her predicament.

"Holly Prentice?" A short Hispanic nurse dressed in hot

pink scrubs called her name. Her small rectangular name tag identified her as Catalina.

"I'm here," Holly said. After she weighed in at one hundred twenty-five pounds, she followed Catalina into the examination room. She hadn't gained any weight. Perhaps this was all in her imagination after all.

"Holly, your test results are in," Catalina said softly while tightening the blood pressure cuff. "The doctor will be here to discuss them with you in a few minutes. Please take everything off from the waist down and cover yourself with this." The nurse handed Holly a paper gown before leaving. Holly undressed, and put her hand on her stomach, wondering if the fluttering she felt was butterflies or her little boy or girl.

Her petite doctor's megawatt smile gave her the answer. "Congratulations!" she trilled.

"Oh, my goodness! I'm pregnant," Holly said more to herself than the doctor. After all these years of waiting for Drew to be ready, and wishing so many times that she was the mother pushing the stroller through the park. She should be happy. So why were tears streaming down her cheeks?

"These are tears of happiness, right?" Dr. Bettencourt asked, handing Holly a tissue.

Unable to speak, Holly nodded, dabbing at her eyes and wiping her running nose. At Dr. Bettencourt's direction, Holly put her feet in the stirrups and tried to relax while the doctor conducted a pelvic examination. The cloth draped around Holly's knees obscured the doctor's face, but they could still carry on a conversation.

"When was your last period?"

"I think it was the last week in August, but I'm not that sure."

"It would be helpful if you could remember, so we can more accurately predict the due date."

Holly smiled ruefully. "That's not a problem, I know the exact date of conception." She told the doctor the date in September.

Dr. Bettencourt snapped off her latex gloves, the examination completed.

"Based on your conception date, I'd say your due date is going to be around May 25th of next year, though first babies are often late." The doctor scribbled something, then handed her a card. "As you've probably figured out, you're about six or seven weeks along.

"Here is the name of an obstetrician I recommend. You should make an appointment right away to set up your prenatal check-ups, and talk about your birthing options." Dr. Bettencourt looked down at the chart. "It doesn't say anything about you being married. Was your divorce finalized? Is there a new guy in the picture?"

"Nick and I… aren't married," Holly said. Aren't really anything to each other—yet, was what she really wanted to say.

"It doesn't matter. I'm sorry if I made you uncomfortable. Look at me," Dr. Bettencourt said gesturing toward her graying hair. "I'm being old fashioned. What I'm asking, rather inartfully, is whether the father, or partner, or whoever will be involved in the pregnancy?" When Holly didn't answer, the doctor continued.

"Even though marriage may be an arcane notion these days, I still think it's important that you get support at a time like this. We like to see the father involved in the process. They can learn a lot coming to these regular check-ups," the doctor said.

Impasse

"To be honest, Dr. Bettencourt, I haven't told him yet. The pregnancy wasn't planned, and our relationship isn't really that solid. I'm not sure what to do. I'm kind of at a loss here."

"Do you want my advice?" Dr. Bettencourt asked. When Holly nodded, she continued. "Tell him." It was a long moment before the doctor spoke again. "From my years of experience, it's better to find out now if he's on board, not when he doesn't show up in the delivery room.

"A baby is stressful on a relationship. It is best for you and for the baby to know if you're on solid ground. But enough preaching," she said, tearing a small page from the pad on the counter. "Here's a prescription for some prenatal vitamins, folic acid, and the like. Follow the instructions on those bottles, but most important, call the OB and get your schedule set. You have a lot of exciting things coming up, including your first sonogram."

During the entire twenty-minute drive home from the doctor's office, Holly replayed the conversation with Dr. Bettencourt in her head. A big part of her wanted to share this, the greatest joy of her life so far, with Nick. In her wildest dreams, it would solidify their relationship, and they could welcome this new person into the world with joy and happiness. But just as the fantasies started to take over, reality set in, and she realized that she was just Holly Prentice, woman on the rebound, pregnant by a twenty-six-year-old guy who didn't own a couch.

When the phone rang later that night, Holly answered it absently, thinking it was Sophie or one of her other work friends inviting her out for a drink or a last minute sushi dinner. Neither of which, she realized now, she could do for a while. Instead, it was Nick.

"I know, I know, I said I wasn't going to call you," Nick said, rushing ahead before she could get in a word of greeting. "But I needed to hear your voice."

Flustered, Holly started talking about work, the only neutral topic she could think of. She gave him a rundown of her latest philanthropic project, a professional clothing drive for women moving from homeless shelters to permanent housing. While they were talking about everything and nothing, and certainly not what they felt for each other, or the fact that she was carrying his baby, Holly, with the phone tucked between her ear and shoulder, sorted through her closet, seeing what gently used suits she could donate to the charity. When the metal rail holding many of her suits crashed to the floor, the phone clattered to the floor as well.

"You okay?" Holly heard Nick's distant voice yelling from the receiver lying on the worn wood planks. Before she could straighten the rack or make sense of the jumble of clothes, she retrieved the phone from the floor. "Nick, I'm fine. I just pushed too much stuff to one side and the closet rod caved in." Holly picked her way through the pile of clothes and pulled the folding doors closed to cover the mess. "I can't deal with this now. Maybe I'll look at it in the morning."

"Are you feeling any better? I really wish I didn't have to leave you while you were sick like that. If these meetings weren't so important…"

"I'm okay, really. I'm feeling a little better every day. Don't worry; I'll be one hundred percent by the time you get back."

"Just leave the clothes for now. I want to talk to you without distractions for a second." Nick's voice had changed, the shift subtle but perceptible.

"You're right, it'll be there in the morning," Holly said as she padded to her bed and propped herself on her frilly, decorative pillows. Until she laid down, she hadn't realized she was exhausted. "So, you coming over?" she said using the sexy invitation he'd gotten used to over the last few weeks.

"Don't tease me like that," Nick said, his voice even huskier than it had been just moments ago. "I feel like Pavlov's dog around you. Just thinking about you is giving me a hard-on." Nick was breathing heavily by now. "What are you wearing?"

"Seriously?" She adopted a playful tone.

"Just tell me." His was not.

"I'm wearing my red silk kimono."

"Anything else?"

"Just panties."

His breathing deepened. "What kind?"

Holly stroked herself lightly through the silk, swept up in the moment as much as Nick. "Just a pair of hot pink bikini panties."

"Open it for me," Nick pleaded. "The kimono, Holly."

"Nick," Holly whispered into the phone, embarrassed by her obvious reaction to his words, even with him more than three thousand miles away.

"Touch yourself. Let me imagine the silk slipping from your body. In my mind, your dusky nipples are pebble-hard, your thighs are parted, waiting for my touch."

As if pulled by invisible marionette strings, Holly complied. She heard the rasp of his zipper through the phone, and imagined Nick stroking himself as slowly and deliberately as she would, reveling in the feel of silk over steel. Instead, at his direction, she stroked herself. His words guided her fingers to pluck her nipples, her hand to her mons, her knuckle to her clitoris.

Nick's rapid breathing and words of encouragement, not to mention her self-manipulation, brought her to the edge then pushed her over. His pleasure came almost simultaneously. In the back of her mind, she thought she heard another declaration of love on the hoarse shout of his satisfaction, but any words that came from his lips were lost in the echoing crescendo of her cries.

The trilling doorbell woke Holly from a dead sleep. She was still a little groggy when she pulled her robe tight around her nude form, wondering who would be calling at this time of day. Sophie knew better than to bother her, especially now with all the fatigue and morning sickness. So she was surprised to see Nick's father, Dominic, standing there sheepishly, toolbox in hand.

Holly tried to act like she hadn't just rolled out of bed at—she looked at her grandmother clock—so named because of its diminutive frame—ten-thirty in the morning.

"Dominic? This is unexpected."

He bustled his way in, not waiting for her invitation. "Nicky called me, said you were getting over a bug. You having some problems with your closet?"

Holly hoped he couldn't see the blood she could feel rushing to her cheeks, thinking about what passed for "conversation" between her and Nick last night. "Um, yeah, kind of. It's not really a problem. It's just that the clothing rod crashed down last night. I didn't put it back because I figured the configuration of my closet is not quite right for the stuff I have in there.

"Did Nick send you here to fix that? It's really not necessary. I was going to get my handyman to do it when he had time."

"No need to call him. I'm here at your disposal all day. Just show me what you need."

Holly showed him the closet in the master bedroom, and left Dominic in the room with tape measure in hand.

After she put on the kettle, she called to him from the kitchen. "I know it's kind of late, but have you eaten breakfast? I could make you a little something."

"I just had some coffee," she heard him say. "I don't want to put you out or anything." Dominic came into the kitchen, notepad in hand, stubby pencil tucked behind his ear. "I have to get a couple of things at the lumber yard."

"Don't worry about it. I'll have something waiting for you when you get back."

When Dominic closed the door, Holly threw off her robe and took a quick shower. By the time Nick's father returned, supplies in hand, she had waffles steaming in the iron. "Come, sit, I've set a place for you. I hope you don't mind tea."

Dominic sat, awkwardly placing her starched, linen napkin in his lap. Watching Holly bustle around the kitchen, he fiddled with the heavy silver she'd laid by his delicate china plate. With a small spatula, Holly lifted the fluffy, steaming waffles from the iron, piled them on his plate, and put a dish of butter and a pitcher of syrup on the table. Filling Dominic's mug, then hers with fragrant tea, she sat down.

"I hope you like the waffles. It's one of my favorite breakfasts."

Dominic wasted no time in tucking into the food. "These are delicious. My Nicky is a lucky man. Aren't you having any?" he asked around a second or third mouthful of the golden waffles.

Holly rubbed her stomach unconsciously. "This, um, bug I've been fighting makes me feel a little sick in the mornings. I'll reheat some a little later."

"I didn't want to put you through any trouble. Nicky would be upset if he knew I had you here working when you're supposed to be resting."

"I'm fine, really. Went to the doctor yesterday. Now eat up."

"So," Dominic said between bites, "how do you like Nicky's house? He did most of the work, you know, my brother and I only helped him out a little. He's quite talented at both rough and finish carpentry."

Holly smiled to herself. Was Dominic touting Nick's good qualities? Little did he know, she was pretty much sold. "I was there last weekend. The place is coming along nicely."

Dominic continued listing Nick's positive attributes like it was a job interview and she was up for the job of "wife."

"I heard you went to that charter school in South L.A. with Nicky as well. Have you seen his films? When he said he didn't want to join his uncle and me, I was disappointed at first, but he's got some real talent. He tells wonderful stories with his films. His mother, Iris, God rest her soul, would so be proud of him." Dominic looked down at his clean plate, chasing a few remaining crumbs with his fork.

"I've seen his documentaries, Dominic. I've always thought he was a better filmmaker than network executive."

"But the best part is that he's not one of those artsy-fartsy types, you know what I mean? He understands how to do his job well, and make a good living from this."

"Nick seems to be doing quite well," Holly said, amused.

Impasse

"You should be very proud of him."

Dominic looked woefully at his empty plate while Holly sipped at her ginger and mint tea, an anti-nausea combination she'd read about on the Internet. He stood up, ready, she assumed, to get to work on the closet, but he spoke again instead. "Holly, I don't know you really well, but you seem like a nice girl who can cook, that's for damn sure. Nick likes you a lot. Maybe he wants to marry you, I don't know. But I'm not getting any younger, and I'm looking forward to enjoying my grandchildren before I get too old to play with them. Are you serious about him?"

Holly felt like a young village woman talking to the sage town matchmaker. Some part of her wanted to shout yes, she wanted Nick forever and all time, and where could she sign up?

How thrilled Dominic would be to find out she was carrying his grandchild. But her brain overruled her heart before she spoke, thank goodness. "Mr. Andreis," Holly said reverting to the formal address, trying to put some distance between herself and this conversation that was getting too close for comfort. "I don't know how to answer you, what you want me to say. Nick and I are just friends… " She trailed off, not sure what else to say to him.

"Maybe I've said too much. I'll just get to that closet. I'm an old man who should not be interfering in the affairs of you young people. Forget I said anything. I'll try not to be too loud. I'll call if I need anything," Dominic said before hightailing it to her bedroom where sawing and hammering began in earnest.

Nick strode purposefully through the offices of HBO. His meeting with the finance people had gone extremely well. His last two completed films had illustrated that he could consistently come in on time and under budget. Helena, on the other hand, had been meeting with people on the creative side, sharing Solstice's vision with the cable network's producers and programmers—showing them that their heartwarming films could appeal to the cable channel's audience.

When Nick heard footsteps approaching, he was taken aback to see Drew Burke approaching. Nick swiftly banished thoughts of last night's heated phone sex with Drew's ex-wife from his head and greeted his mentor warmly.

"It's great to see you in New York," Drew said, clasping Nick's hand and pulling him in for a brief male embrace. "I'm glad I was able to help you set up these meetings. Is it good news? Will Solstice be doing something with HBO?"

"Helena and I are hoping they'll co-produce a new documentary we're starting to film in the spring."

"That's great," Drew said sincerely. "Shoot me an e-mail and let me know everyone you're meeting with. I'll put in a good word for you, follow up on the project, make sure it doesn't languish in development."

They talked a little more about Solstice's plans and the real likelihood that Drew would be moving to Manhattan permanently. Nick knew, however, their conversation wasn't over. As a stand-up guy, he knew he needed to broach the issue of his relationship with Holly.

"Drew, do you have a minute? I need to discuss something kind of personal."

Drew glanced at his watch and led Nick toward a small conference area with two leather chairs and a small chrome and glass table.

"I'm here to help. I may not have thought you leaving the network was smart—you could have gone really far there—but I still think you have a great career ahead of you. So what gives?"

Nick paused. Solstice Entertainment meant a lot not only to him but to Helena as well. He didn't want his feelings for Holly to cloud his judgment, but he didn't want his relationship with Drew to be clouded by half-truths either.

"This doesn't have to do with work. This has to do with Holly."

"My ex?"

Nick looked down at his hands searching for the right words then looked Drew straight in the eye. "Drew, we've been seeing each other for a couple of months, and things are getting pretty serious. I'm not seeking your approval by any means. Holly and I are both adults and can make our own decisions. I'm just telling you this man to man, because I want our business relationship to be honest and above board. I'll completely understand if this means you don't lend your full support to our projects here."

Helena would pick that delicate moment to turn the corner and approach their conversation.

"Drew," she enthused. He stood to embrace and greet her. "It's great to see you. Has Nick gotten you caught up on our latest film? We're pretty keyed up about working with an established cable network. It'll be great to know the funding is there as well as a built-in audience for the documentary once it's complete..." Helena looked from one man to another.

Nick stood. "Helena, I was telling Drew about me and Holly."

"Oh," Helena said, promptly falling into the seat Nick had just vacated.

All three were quiet for a few minutes until Drew broke the silence.

"Well, good luck to you then. I'll be talking to you soon," he said, then walked away down the long corridor, never once looking back at them.

Helena sank back in the plush leather seat, looking resigned. "So, what did that mean?"

Nick sank back into his chair as well, his posture mirroring Helena's. "I wish I knew."

"Hey, Nicky," Holly said a teasing note in her voice, when she answered his call.

"Ah, my dad came by."

"Nick, I don't know how to thank you. He did a great job. He dismantled everything and re-did the entire interior in cedar. It looks good and smells good to boot."

"Dad's great." There was a pause on the line. They experienced an awkwardness that hadn't ever been present between them before. It took everything in Holly not to shout out to him that they were having a baby.

"Holly, are you feeling better?" Nick eventually asked, no doubt his attempt to ease the tension between them.

"I'm better," Holly said vaguely, not wanting to invite too many questions about her "stomach flu."

She heard what she thought was a sigh. "I really miss you. In every meeting, on every conference call, I've been distracted thinking about you. I want nothing more than to come back and hold you, kiss you, make love to you."

"Nick, I don't know what you want me to say. I want those

things too, I just don't know if we can have them."

He paused, absorbing her words. "Holly, I know we weren't going to talk about any of this while I was away, but I've said it once and I'm going to say it again. I love you. I've been dancing around it for weeks trying not to make you feel uncomfortable, not to put any pressure on you. But I have to be true to myself, and more than anything, I want you to want to be with me."

This pause was even longer. Holly could hear the static from Nick's cell crackle in the silence. "Nick, I—I need more time." Now with the baby looming in her mind, Holly truly couldn't say whether she loved Nick or was just infatuated with the idea of being with him—giving her baby a father and a home.

Nine

"I'm coming!" Holly called out to the visitor knocking on her front door. She'd never been this popular. Before September, she could count on her hand the number of times she had unexpected night visitors. Surely her neighbors thought she was some kind of girl gone wild. Since Nick was in New York, Sophie would never stop by without calling first, and she couldn't think of any screw or hinge Dominic had left untightened, Holly was at a loss as to who could be at her door this evening. Maybe it was Nick's dad again, trying to sell her on the virtues of his son or coming to work some other carpentry miracle. She could only hope for the latter.

Holly pulled open the door before the person could rap the iron knocker again, and was shocked to see Drew filling her doorframe. She had to admit he looked good. His once shaggy hair was now in an executive cut, neat and well groomed. A tan that couldn't have been natural graced what she could see of him. Divorce became him, she guessed. But for some reason, her stomach didn't do flip-flops like it did with Nick. He was still handsome in his own right, but whatever attraction they'd shared in the past was no longer there, much to her relief.

It had been forever since they'd talked face to face, though they'd spoken on the phone or gotten in touch by email to settle what few remaining financial matters they still had. She invited him in, amazed that she no longer felt that pull like in the early days of their relationship, nor did she feel any of the anger she'd held for so many months or the disappointment at his cavalier attitude toward the end of their marriage.

"This is unexpected," Holly said, stepping back to let Drew into the apartment. He strode in like he owned the place, confident as always. Something about his proprietary nature made her the slightest bit uneasy. "Not to be rude, but why are you here?"

He grabbed her hands in his and sat down on her settee, pulling her with him. Holly didn't pull her hands from his right away, even though, somehow, his touch felt wrong. They had been married once upon a time. She would like them to be something akin to friends.

"Holly." He paused looking at her in a way he hadn't looked at her in probably a decade. Soberly, he said, "I'm moving to New York, permanently."

"Are congratulations in order?" she asked trying to suss out his motives.

"Actually, yes." Drew smiled warmly. "I'll be starting in January as vice president of daytime programming."

"Have you ever watched a soap opera or a talk show?"

"No, not yet, but it's a good opportunity. Daytime ratings are terrible. If I can turn that around and attract the very desirable younger audience all networks are looking for, then I've been promised a crack at prime time in a couple of years.

"Well then, congratulations!" Holly said more animatedly than was warranted. "But you could have just emailed me your new address. I think we've sorted out almost all of our matters. The bank can send you your half of the certificates of deposit that come due."

"I want you to come with me."

"Where?" Holly said, ignorant of his meaning for a long moment. "Oh, New York."

She was flabbergasted. Of all the things she could have imagined coming from Drew, this was the absolute last. His offhand attitude toward their divorce—and their marriage, frankly—had led her to believe that their whole relationship had meant very little to him. When Holly said her vows those many years ago, she assumed death would be the only way their union would end.

Looking at the country's divorce statistics, she realized she'd had stars in her eyes. Now she was much wiser. Holly pulled her hands from his and stood up to pace the room. "Drew, why this? Why now?"

He closed his eyes and bowed his head, resting his chin on his steepled fingers for a few moments, gathering his thoughts. "I realize that I never stopped loving you. I was wrong to think we couldn't have it all. I want us back. I promise, I'll work less. I'm ready now to start that family you've always wanted."

Holly sunk to the floor where she'd been standing across the room from Drew, leaning her back against the rough-hewn entry door.

Drew rushed over to her from the couch and crouched down next to her. "Are you okay?" He sank down, and fumbled with something in his pocket. To her surprise a small velvet box emerged. Shit. This wasn't going to end well. She could definitely see that. When he opened the box, she gasped.

"Holly, give me a second chance," he said as she gaped at the ring.

"Drew, where did you get this? It's just like my grandmother's." Her grandmother's ring had been a family heirloom that had gone missing. Even with careful prodding, her grandmother would never reveal what had happened to the ring, but Holly suspected she'd had to pawn it during one of her grandfather's business downturns. Despite the ring's disappearance, there were a few pictures of her grandmother showing off the ring at parties in the nineteen twenties, dressed in her flapper finery.

"I knew you always loved that ring. I had a jeweler in Beverly Hills replicate it for you. You never liked the other one I gave you—I know now it was too ostentatious; four carats on your small hand, I can't imagine what I was thinking—but this one is just right for you, just right for us. The new 'us' going forward."

Drew leaned against the door next to her, and he thrust the open box into her hands. She pulled the ring from the box. It was beautiful. No, it was exquisite. It was an art deco styled ring, the diamond set in a platinum band. The stone was square cut, clear, and beautiful. The band was meticulously mill grained with intricate inlaid designs. She looked at Drew. Where was this man five years ago, even two years ago? Now, staring into his earnest, handsome face, all she could think of was Nick.

She put the ring back in its velvet case and set it on the wood floor in the small space between them. "Drew. This, all of this. I don't know what to say."

"Say yes."

Holly shifted, pulling her knees up to her chest and resting her head there. "Why are you here? You don't want me or this," Holly said gesturing to the room around her. "How did you know I was seeing someone?"

"Why do you… " Drew's shoulders lifted, his hands reaching out palms up.

"I've known you for more than ten years. You always went after the thing you couldn't have. When that first HR executive at NBC said you would never succeed in television, you worked like hell to get a job and thrived in television."

"I ran into Nick Andreis in New York this week. Until I came face to face with someone you were dating, I don't think I realized it was really over."

"What did Nick say to you exactly?" Holly said slowly, simmering, trying not to let her renewed anger boil over.

"He thought I should know that you two were seeing each other."

"He thought you should know? Drew, my private life is now private, and that excludes you. I don't appreciate you and Nick discussing me like some television deal." Holly blew out an exasperated breath. "What you guys said to each other doesn't matter. Drew, maybe we could have salvaged things before the divorce, but it's too late. And not just because of Nick, but because of the 'us' that won't ever be again."

Drew was quiet for a long time. He said softly, "Then you should know that he loves you, Holly. I mean really loves you. When he was talking about you in New York, I wished I could have loved you that deeply. I wanted a chance to do us over. But you deserve the life you want. A man who loves you above all else, the family you've always wanted. Until a few minutes ago, I thought I could be that man again. I came here hoping you'd give me a second chance."

"I'm pregnant, Drew," Holly interjected, attempting to put a definitive end to his fantasies of them playing house ever again.

"I guess I'm not the only person who deserves congratulations," Drew said. Then he looked at her, really looked at her. "Is it Nick's?"

Holly looked down at her hands, bare of anyone's ring.

"Yes, of course he's the father. I don't even know why I told you this. He doesn't know, yet. Please don't mention it to him if you see him."

Drew gestured toward the ring box still on the floor between them. "Are you two getting married?"

"No, Drew. I'm off marriage right now. As you know, the last one didn't work out too well even though I put my all into it."

"Touché," he said, chagrined.

He stood, straightening his logo emblazoned cashmere pullover. He pulled Holly to her feet. She accepted one last hug from Drew. "If I can do anything to help you, all you have to do is call."

Ten

Nick was coming home today, Holly practically crowed to herself. Her jubilation was evident in the bounce in her step and the smile she couldn't suppress. Even when she tried to hide her anticipation behind her usually cool demeanor, excitement bubbled out and she danced a little jig.

When Nick had phoned last night, it had been a welcome surprise. After those first two nights of emotional and steamy calls, he'd been as good as his original word. It had been three long weeks since Nick left for New York City—two weeks longer than he intended. When she counted, which she wouldn't admit to anyone, there had been almost three whole weeks of telephone silence from Nick. Though she'd asked for it to be that way, being without Nick, even his voice, had been hard. She'd made that tentative first call and scheduled her first obstetrician appointment alone, made plans for her baby alone, and slept alone. It was indeed good news that tonight, if she played her cards right, she wouldn't be sleeping by herself—or even sleeping at all.

Even though she had missed him terribly, she hadn't wasted their time apart. Holly had used the weeks to think about the baby she was going to raise and what Nick meant to her. Nick apparently had used their time apart productively as well. He'd emailed her HBO had picked up Solstice's project. Not wanting to lose momentum, Nick said that he and Helena had spent the past two weeks ironing out the contractual details with the network and lining up interview subjects for the documentary they would film in the coming spring and summer months.

So, while Nick had been working, she'd had time to think about whether she wanted a "them." After being constantly preoccupied with thoughts of their budding relationship and of the life burgeoning in her womb, she'd decided that she was willing to try a more permanent relationship with Nick. Though she still hadn't decided how to tell him about their child. Almost ten weeks along, she was certainly going to have to figure out a way to break the news to him before he figured it out from just looking at her. If all went well, she could tell him about the baby tonight.

Shaking her head to clear it of all these thoughts, a newfound sense of energy and urgency surged through Holly. She wanted to do something special for Nick's return. Suddenly an idea came to her and she grabbed the phone.

Her main focus was to welcome Nick home with a homemade dinner by candlelight, but that was just part of the evening. It had taken three of them—herself, Sophie, and Dominic—the better part of Saturday to put the whole thing together, and she only hoped she could pull this off without giving Nick a heart attack. She knew from living alone that a real live person showing up in your home could be scary.

The problem with her spur-of-the-moment brainstorm had been twofold: first, as much as she loved her apartment, she had no real dining room and nowhere to put her grandmother's dining room table, currently in storage. Of course, Nick had a dining room but no table—which was where Dominic and Sophie had come in. Nick's dad had assured her Nick would welcome the idea of her waiting for him at his house and had given her a spare set of keys.

Then the three of them had squeezed into the front cab of Dominic's pickup and driven over to her storage space. With considerable effort and a lot of care, they were able to load her antique refectory table, rescued from a now defunct monastery, and silk damask dining room chairs into his truck. The harder part was getting the large table up the narrow entry stairs of Nick's house and situated in the dining area. When they were done, Dominic and Sophie had to admit it had been worth all the effort. The table fit perfectly.

The sturdy elm table, its aged patina thick with years of lovingly applied furniture oil, fit the rustic looking interior beautifully. The chandelier, which had come with the house, had verdigris that complimented the antique furniture. The chairs, though faded with time, lent an air of elegance to the room. When Nick's dad offered to take Sophie for sandwiches and then home, Holly was relieved. Looking at her watch, she realized she had only six hours to go shopping and pull together something scrumptious for dinner.

Impasse

As dusk fell, she heard Nick's limo pull up outside, and she was ready. The lights were dimmed, the fireplace and candles were lit. After spending far too much time at the gourmet food market caught up in indecision, Holly had decided on a simple French provincial meal.

She poached a small whole salmon, served with her special Dijon mayonnaise, and made a squash gratin generously sprinkled with gruyere cheese. After decanting a Côtes-du-Rhone, Holly mopped her brow with the striped kitchen towel and out of habit started to relax with a small glass of wine at the dining room table. She caught herself before taking a sip and poured the wine down the sink, happy that she had a reason to refrain from drinking. She hadn't managed dessert, but she figured they'd worry about that later, if at all.

"What the… " she heard Nick growl as he banged his heavy luggage up the stairs.

"Nick? It's me," Holly said, tentatively.

Nick walked into the dimly lit living room, and Holly held her breath. She needn't have worried, not one second really, because Nick dropped his bags and rushed forward to gather her up in his arms. It felt achingly familiar, and it felt good, very good. It felt right. As she stood there, first hugging, then kissing Nick with all she had, Holly knew she'd made the right decision. When they finally broke apart, Holly started talking rapidly, still trying to work off the nerves she was feeling about this very special night with him.

"I hope you don't mind. I kind of got the idea to surprise you with dinner, and borrowed the keys from your dad. Then I realized you didn't have a table, so I brought mine over. I hope you like salmon, because that's what's for dinner. I'm keeping the squash warm in the—" Holly stopped speaking when Nick covered her lips with his finger, causing a long shiver to course through her body.

"Shhhh. Holly, it's more than okay," Nick said, removing his finger from her lips. "This is the best thing I could hope for after three lonely weeks in New York and a long day of cross-country travel." He ran his work-roughened hands along her face and down her arms, finally grasping her hands in his. "I hope this means what I think it means, that you've decided to give us a chance."

Overcome with a rush of emotion that constricted her throat, muting her, Holly could only nod. Nick gave her one last quick kiss, which stole what breath she had left.

"So, what's for dinner? And where did this great table come from?"

When he talked about anything other than their relationship, Holly relaxed. To her greater relief, Nick loved the food, and she felt even calmer after his second glass of wine. She told him what she knew of the history of the table, her late grandfather having come by during a trip to a small town in France. Learning the monastery was closing, he purchased the handmade elm table for a few francs and had it shipped to the United States by freighter. The table took longer to arrive than he did, but she fondly remembered many meals, homework sessions, and earnest conversations at the table with her grandmother.

Famished after hours of scant airplane food, Nick made short work of the salmon and gratin. Holly only toyed with her food, more hungry for Nick than sustenance. If he noticed her drinking water instead of wine, he didn't say anything.

"I missed you these last years," he finally said.

Holly, disconcerted by Nick's sudden change in tone, asked, "What do you mean?"

"Don't tell me you've forgotten our tradition."

"Nick, we don't have any traditions." Other than screwing each other's brains out, she thought.

"I think this table would be perfect for Thanksgiving."

"Thanksgiving?"

"I had to celebrate it without you. It just wasn't the same. Asha and Hayes may throw a great party, but shaking martinis isn't cooking. We did a passable job, but the turkey was dry and the gravy was lumpy."

"You just want me for my giblets, don't you?"

Nick laughed. "What did you do last year?"

Holly had spent the past year, and the one before that alone. She hadn't been ready to pretend she was okay. The idea of a get together reminded her too much of what she'd lost with her divorce: her friends, her sense of belonging. Holly snapped from her reverie when she felt Nick's warm hand envelop hers on the table.

"It doesn't matter what you did last year—it's all in the past. Let's do it here this year."

"Turkey day? Are you sure? There will be tons of food, all our friends, you know how hectic it can be."

Nick looked positively jubilant at the idea. "I'll help. We'll have Sophie, my dad, Asha and Hayes, Helena, some of my friends from the network." With the mention of Drew's and Nick's old employer, he paused. "It's okay if we have some of the folks from the network, isn't it? They used to enjoy coming to your celebrations."

Holly didn't respond right away. It wasn't the network folks that bothered her, per se. It was the fact that their friends, her and Drew's old acquaintances, would see them as a couple. There would be no going back.

"Okay, we'll do it!" Holly said, shaking off any sense of trepidation. Holly could feel her curls bouncing around her face. "But remember, you promised to help. I'll be holding you to that—no running off to watch the game."

After she cleared the plates, she rejoined Nick at the table, sitting next to him, this time turned sideways in her chair facing him, inhaling his clean, masculine scent—something else she hadn't realized she missed.

When she would have spoken, Nick framed her face with his strong hands, his fingers caught in her spiral curls.

"God, I missed you. This. Us. I know we haven't spoken of this in weeks; I love you, Holly." When she attempted to break eye contact with him, he lifted her chin gently, until he could look directly into her eyes. "You have to trust my feelings for you. I don't plan to go anywhere. I don't want anyone other than you. Let me show you how I feel. Let me make love with you."

He kissed her then, slipping from tenderness to want to stark need in what seemed like milliseconds. Before she could process what was happening, Nick had lifted Holly so that she was straddling him, sitting on his lap. When he broke the kiss to look into her eyes, there was no mistaking the love he felt for her.

At the juncture of her thighs, Holly could also feel the hard evidence of his desire. Though the first two were already undone, Nick unbuttoned the last two fasteners of her Henley knit, exposing the tops of her breasts and cleavage to his greedy gaze. When looking wasn't enough, Nick slid his hands along her smooth back, under her shirt, gently lifting the caramel knit top over her head. Her unfettered breasts came free, and he gently cupped them in his hands.

Glad that the early pregnancy tenderness had abated somewhat, Holly reveled in his touch. If Nick noticed her recently engorged breasts, he didn't say anything. He slid the roughened pads of his thumbs against her ultra-sensitive nipples. Holly almost came right then. Never had a man's touch on her breasts sent her to such dizzying heights of bliss. Unable to suppress her cry of pleasure, Holly fell ravenously upon his lips, upping the heat intensity between them about ten notches.

She pulled his striped green polo over his head, making them both naked to the waist. When rubbing her silk-encased clit against his erection wasn't enough, Holly lifted her short skirt to get closer to him. Letting go of her breasts and untangling his fingers from her hair, Nick pulled open the button fly of his jeans, and pushed his briefs aside, springing his hard cock from its confines. Licking her lips in anticipation, Holly stepped away only long enough to discard the wisp of her silk panties, sat astride him, and with no preamble whatsoever enveloped his throbbing penis inside her.

"Holly," he gasped, trying to stop himself from driving into her, "we're not protected."

She realized then the mistake she had made.

"It's okay," Holly said, a Mona Lisa smile playing around her lips.

Nick thrust involuntarily, presumably unable to stop himself from the sheer pleasure.

"Are you sure?"

When she nodded almost solemnly, Nick didn't question her further. He let go, losing any semblance of control. His hands spanned her waist, guiding her along his length. Reflexively, he pistoned into her. Holly matched him thrust for thrust. The angle of their joining was such that the friction against her sensitive nub caused her to come not once, but twice—the second time so hard that for a few seconds she lost all sense of time and space.

When their breathing quieted once again, neither moved to separate their bodies. Even without words, their bond remained strong, like a taut electrical wire zinging current between them. Nick caressed her hair, her neck, her lips, while her arms looped loosely around his neck, their intense stare unbroken. Holly couldn't think of any time better than now to tell him about their baby to be. She looked down involuntarily, gathering her resolve.

Their eye contact broken, they both started to speak simultaneously. She let him speak first. "Holly, I can't seem to control myself when it comes to making love with you."

She shushed him, overflowing with her joy and excitement. "Nick, it's nothing. I'm one hundred percent sure we're okay," she said with a smile, her heart brimming with the secret she was ready to spill.

His eyes closed for a heartbeat, then stared directly into hers. "Holly, it's not that I don't want children, want a family with you someday, but I'm looking forward to getting to really know you—building a solid foundation for our future—before we have to worry about children."

Impasse

Holly deflated at Nick's words. All her joy and happiness evaporated like so much helium from a burst balloon. She eased herself from Nick and excused herself, walking upstairs to the bathroom with her discarded clothing. Nick had adjusted himself when she returned fully dressed, though he remained shirtless with the top two buttons of his denim fly undone. Looking at Nick and loving him—for she was finally able to admit to herself it was love—Holly tried to hide her trembling lower lip. Turning away, ostensibly looking out the front windows into the inky blackness of the canyon night, she impatiently brushed away the traitorous tears from her eyes.

"I have to go, Nick," she whispered.

"Why?"

"This is just… Nick, I need time to think, that's all." She grabbed her purse and her key ring, still heavy with the addition of Nick's keys, and ran out the door.

Holly managed to hold in her tears until she was safely behind her locked apartment door. Then she cried, uninhibited. It was Drew all over again. Nick wanted her but not her baby. She'd given up her dreams once for a man, but not this time. She loved Nick, but she loved her baby-to-be more.

Nick stalked around his house, bare-chested, hands raking through his hair, trying to figure out Holly. His dad had claimed to never understand women and apparently that particular trait was hereditary. One moment Holly was the sexy siren he'd always fantasized about, then the next minute she'd gone cold. And to his way of thinking, he hadn't said or done anything to cause her abrupt shift in mood.

Just when things were finally going right. Holly ran, and he was always chasing her. Nick had been more than happy to see Holly at his home where she belonged. Her bringing the table had signified a huge step in their relationship. Holly had lent him a family heirloom, clearly precious to her.

She'd cooked him a delicious meal. She'd made love to him like a siren, temporarily fulfilling his ravenous appetite for her. She hadn't told him she loved him in so many words, but he felt her love in the myriad ways she'd tried to please him. He wanted to marry her someday, but he felt like he was back at square one again. Someday was looking like it was never going to come.

Nick jogged up the stairs to his bedroom to grab a long-sleeved tee and fleece jacket to ward against the night chill. She'd had enough time alone. The running, the withholding, the rules. It was all over. They were a couple now, and they would start figuring things out together. He pulled on his shoes, grabbed his keys, and headed out the door.

Bottom line: she was worth chasing.

He was tired, damn tired with jet lag, but getting to the bottom of the murky waters that constantly swirled around his relationship with Holly was more important than a good night's sleep. Maybe there was something to that expression "you can sleep when you're dead." He couldn't see his love for Holly abating any sooner than that. The sound of her crying just beyond the thick wood door only increased his urgency.

"Holly!" he shouted, pounding on the door.

He heard a muffled response, but before he could knock again, Holly pulled it open. Her blotched face caused his heart to leap directly to his throat. When he pulled her into his arms, his thoughts were anything but sexual. He wanted to comfort this woman that he loved, however he could.

"Holly, whatever's wrong, we can fix it," Nick said, leading her to the bedroom. He helped her strip down to her silky under things, and tucked her into the large bed. "I promise."

Nick disrobed, keeping his boxer-briefs on for once, and got into the bed with her. He gathered her into his arms. Her sobs had subsided, but she breathed unsteadily into his chest.

"What's going on?" he asked, whispering into her strawberry scented hair, bracing himself for anything.

"I'm pregnant," she said. "We're going to have a baby."

But not that.

Nick was silent for some time. He was sure Holly could feel the sudden thudding of his heart where her head lay on his chest.

"When?" He reflexively wanted to ask "how" as well, but given the many times and ways they'd been together, that answer was obvious.

"It was that first time, after the graduation—when we got carried away."

"But that was in September. How far along…"

"About ten weeks now."

"When did you—"

Holly sat up abruptly, interrupting Nick. The covers pooled around her hips, her preoccupation making her impervious to the night's chill pebbling her nipples under her sheer camisole. "Sophie started suspecting when I got sick right before you left for New York. She insisted that I take a pregnancy test that night. It was positive. As soon as I could get an appointment, I went to my doctor, and she confirmed it. My first appointment with the

OB is next week."

Suddenly it hit Nick. Shit. He'd rhapsodized about wanting time with Holly alone before they thought about children. No doubt that comment had sent her racing from his house. As the silence between them stretched, Holly shifted again.

"Nick, I know this is a lot to get your head around, and I've had more time than you to get used to it. I'm not expecting anything from you, so let's just call it a night."

Her lack of faith in him arrowed straight to his heart. Emotionally and physically exhausted himself, Nick agreed to sleep for now and talk later. When Holly would have curled up into herself, Nick fitted himself against her back, his arm and large hand molded against her stomach, which he realized was just slightly rounded. He wondered what other changes he may have noticed in his lover's body had he not been blinded by lust that evening. As their breathing lengthened and evened, Nick whispered into her hair, "I love you more than you know."

When the rosy fingertips of dawn caressed Holly's cheek, she felt Nick stir beside her. She turned to look into his sleepy, green eyes and they communicated wordlessly. Without breaking eye contact, she skimmed her camisole over her head and shimmied from her silk panties. Nick shucked his boxer briefs, and their lips melded in a kiss that was more simmer than burn.

Nick caressed her face, moving the hair aside to touch her delicate ears. He stroked her eyebrows and lips, moving to her slim neck to finger the filigreed silver locket she often wore.

"Do you feel any different—your body, I mean?"

Impasse

She nodded. "I've been really tired and nauseous a lot, but that's subsiding, which is good."

Nick skimmed the pads of his fingers along the delicate blue veins that now showed in her breasts.

Holly's breathing quickened and Nick jerked his fingers away. She grasped his hands and laid them upon her breasts again.

"Is it okay that I touch you there?"

"It's more than okay. Just be gentle. My nipples have been extra sensitive."

"Is that good or bad?" Nick asked, lightly brushing his fingers against the hardened nubbins as she gasped in pure pleasure.

"It's bad in the sense that there's sometimes chafing during the day—I wear a really soft cotton bra when I wear one at all. But it's good in the sense that I think I'll come apart if you keep touching them like you are."

He removed his hands from her breasts and smoothed them along the slightly convex curve of her stomach. Though his touch was light, his breathing was anything but.

"What does it feel like inside? Does it hurt?"

"So far, it feels a little like butterflies in my stomach—but that may just be the morning sickness. It doesn't hurt at all though."

"Can you… I mean, can we still?"

"The doctor said it's perfectly okay. And with all of these hormones running through my body, I've been horny as hell."

She let him take the lead then, and basked in his kiss, his caress. They made slow, languorous love that morning, and Holly tried not to dwell on the fact that it felt like goodbye.

When they parted, Nick reached over to her nightstand to turn down her radio, which had come on at the usual time, knocking off the velvet box Drew had left in her apartment. Picking up the box, he opened it curiously.

"What's this?" he asked.

"It's from Drew."

Nick looked at her, clearly perplexed. "Drew Burke?"

"He left it for me when he came by a couple of weeks ago."

"But he's in New York."

"He was. He's moving there permanently. I don't know how to say this, Nick, so I'll just say it. He wanted us to get back together. He proposed marriage again, family, the whole shebang."

Usually so laid back, worry etched Nick's face. "Are you considering it?"

Holly closed her eyes and slowly shook her head. "No, Nick. He knows about us. I told him about the baby."

Nick's voice was hoarse when he next spoke. "Why did you tell him but not me?"

"It wasn't like that, Nick. I did it without thinking. We used to be married. I'm… I was in the habit of telling him everything. It just seemed the easiest way to show him that he and I were over forever. Nick, I don't want Drew back. You have to believe that."

"Do you want me instead?"

Holly countered his question with one of her own. "Will you take the both of us?"

"Holly…"

"It's a package deal, Nick. It's all or nothing for me."

"I don't… I can't make a decision like this on the spot."

"Nor would I expect you to," Holly said, though she really did and his hesitation was a huge blow to her burgeoning love for him. She didn't know if she could trust her heart to someone

Impasse

who couldn't commit.

Unselfconscious for once and uncaring about her nudity, Holly slid from the bed and fished around in her bedside nightstand. Finding a piece of paper and a pen, she jotted down some notes.

"Here's the date and time of my first obstetrician appointment. It's at Cedars-Sinai. If you can make it… " Holly didn't finish her thought. She thrust the paper at Nick and walked to the bathroom, slamming the door. It was clear, for this morning at least, the conversation was over.

Someday had turned into today. Nick sat in the confined space of the two-seater Mercedes for a long time. A baby. A freaking baby. With crying, and diapers, and daycare, and preschool. He didn't know a damn thing about any of it. Fatherhood was a mystery.

Marriage and family, and kids had always been some far off fantasy. Sure, he wanted what his parents had, but he didn't know if he was ready to do it now. God, in his mind, he'd imagined dating Holly for a couple of years at least to make sure they were compatible for the long term. Surely, they'd get their fill of one another, and he wanted to be with her when sex wasn't the most prominent thing on his mind. Then, maybe they'd get engaged, then married. Babies had seemed as real as winning an Oscar.

Nick counted on his fingers. Holly could give birth in May or June. Where would he be? He rarely filmed exclusively in Los Angeles. He could be in New York, or Europe, or even Africa following a story. How would they bring a baby to far flung parts of the world? Would she and the baby stay behind? How could he be a father if he wasn't ever home? Holly was an adult and they were mature enough that their relationship could handle separations. But how could he explain to a two-month-old, or a two-year-old that Daddy had to go out of town—to make a living?

Daddy. Some little boy or girl would call him Daddy.

Time to think, that's what he needed. How could Holly be so sure of her decision when he was so shaky?

Eleven

Though Holly and Nick were still together, in a manner of speaking, their relationship hadn't progressed from the night she told him about the baby. They still saw each other almost every night because, despite the wall her pregnancy put between them, they hadn't been able to slake their desire for one another.

Hormones were running through her body like wildfire through the California brush. She didn't know if she couldn't get enough of Nick or of sex with Nick, but their almost nightly romps kept her going from day to day. As long as their passion was as strong as ever, the proverbial elephant in the living room, her pregnancy, got short shrift in the mix. When they had been together last night, this morning's appointment hadn't come up. Talking wasn't their main activity.

Yes, the last two weeks had been a holding pattern, but in her eyes this was the true test. If Nick didn't come to the appointment today, then she had decided to break it off once and for all. There was no need, really, to keep on going the way they were. It would only make it harder later.

Pushing open the doctor's hall door to reveal the antiseptic waiting room, Holly's heart sunk to the pit of her stomach like a stone in a shallow lake. Nick wasn't there. As far as she could see into the future, it was all over except for the messy breakup she desperately wanted to avoid.

She made herself comfortable as she filled out the questionnaire the receptionist had handed her on a clipboard. Every time the door to the obstetrician's office opened, Holly's heart jumped to her throat. Was Nick merely late? The first time the door swung it was a young mother with an older woman, likely her mother. For the first time in a long time, Holly acutely missed having a mother. The second time it opened, Holly had to swallow down the lump in her throat. Everyone there reminded her of what she didn't have.

It was a young couple, obviously enchanted with each other, who looked as if they were sharing the woman's first pregnancy together. Resigned to going it alone, Holly finished the survey and prepared to soldier through this first appointment. She was just getting ready to dial Sophie on her cell to get her acquiescence on acting as a birth coach when an older nurse called her name.

The lobby door and the door to the doctor's inner sanctum opened simultaneously, causing a momentary wind vacuum, which swept Holly's hair about. Just as she turned to follow the nurse, Nick strode purposefully through the door. "I'm sorry I'm late—Helena and I were in the editing bay trying to get a promo package out to New York before the overnight shipping deadline."

Impasse

Holly wasn't sure if the relief showed on her face, but hope burgeoned anew. They followed the nurse to the examining room, Nick bringing up the rear of their little group. The nurse took her blood pressure and asked a few perfunctory questions that Holly answered automatically.

"Undress completely and put on this gown. The doctor will be performing a pelvic and breast exam during this first visit. Your husband—"

"Nick's not… " Holly stuttered, not sure what to say. "We're not married."

The nurse nodded understandingly, not pausing a beat. "The baby's father—did you say the name was Nick?" she asked, addressing him directly. "You can accompany the mom-to-be during the examination if you both feel comfortable with that."

Nick merely nodded and sat on a stool placed near the head of the examination table. When the nurse left them alone, plunking her chart in a plastic bin on the door, Holly rose to begin undressing. His hand on her arm caused her to pause. "Do you want me to stay?"

"I really would like that, yes," Holly said, disrobing. Almost reflexively, Nick reached out to stroke her nipple, peaked in the cold examination room. He pulled his hand back before he touched her, probably realizing it was an inappropriate setting for that.

The squeak of the doctor's shoes on the clean linoleum floor hurried Holly's movements, and she covered herself with the paper gown, tying the insubstantial plastic belt around her waist.

"Good morning, Holly," the dark haired young doctor said, shaking her hand. "I'm Dr. Sebastian Cole. And you are?" he asked, extending his hand toward Nick.

"Nick Andreis. I'm the baby's father," he said, stumbling over the words.

"Good to meet you. Holly, here's what's going to happen today. I'm going to get a detailed family history and ask you about your first few weeks of pregnancy. Then I'm going to conduct a pelvic exam. If you have questions at any time. just ask." He looked at Nick. "That goes for both of you."

Dr. Cole started with the standard questions: her parents' health, the date of her last menstruation, the date of conception, and how she felt. Holly told him about her fatigue and morning sickness, leaving out the part about being horny all the time.

"Have you ever been pregnant before?"

Holly hesitated only a moment before answering, "Yes, once."

Though Holly heard Nick's swift intake of breath, she didn't meet his gaze. She continued to look only at Dr. Cole, then the floor.

"Did the pregnancy come to term?"

"No, I had a miscarriage at about fourteen weeks."

"Did the doctor diagnose a cause?"

"Not really. We discussed possible chromosomal abnormalities. But, she explained that it could be just 'one of those things.' I think that it was due, in part at least, to the stress the pregnancy put on my marriage. I really wanted the baby, and my ex-husband didn't. I think we argued about it most nights right up until the miscarriage."

Looking genuinely concerned, Dr. Cole scooted forward on his wheeled stool and took Holly's ice cold hands in his. "You should know that each and every pregnancy is different. There is often nothing that can be done to prevent a miscarriage. The best thing you can do is take care of yourself. Eat well. Get plenty of rest. Just follow the instructions that I'll give you today, and do what feels right."

Holly nodded, trying to swallow back her tears. Nick, didn't move from where he sat, seemingly rooted to the spot near the head of the examination table. Dr. Cole stood. "The nurse will be in to prep you for the pelvic examination. I'll be back in a few minutes."

As soon as the door closed behind him, Nick spoke. "Holly, I didn't know. I'm so sorry," he said, his voice hoarse with concern.

"It's okay. Only Drew and Sophie know. I don't like to revisit that time in my life."

Holly lay back on the examination table as the nurse came in and bustled about, placing her feet in the stirrups and getting the implements ready for the doctor.

"After your exam," the nurse said, "I'll take you down to the lab, and we'll get the blood and urine samples there. If anything comes up, our office will call you. For now, just relax. The doc will do a Pap smear and all the same things as a regular pelvic exam." She looked at Nick sympathetically. "You can stay if you want, but most men are a little squeamish about this part."

When the nurse left, Nick took Holly's still cold hands in his, rubbing them briskly to warm them up in the clinically cold room. "Do you want me to stay?"

Yes, Holly thought. Instead she said, "It's pretty routine from here on out. If you have somewhere to be, it's okay to go. This exam and the blood test can get pretty gruesome," she said reasonably, putting all the gaiety in her voice that she could muster. All her fantasies of babies and families and settling down aside, Holly knew it was time to let him go. She needed someone who was in one hundred percent, not someone who'd come out of obligation.

Nick hesitated for a moment, and Holly's heart leapt to her throat, hope blossoming there.

"If it's okay, I have some stuff I could be working on back at the studio." Nick looked at his watch. "But I'll call you later to see how it went," he said, distracted. He checked his phone, his thumb working the tiny controls. He had checked out before he'd even left the room.

Just as quickly as it had bloomed, that hope died. Her fantasies of him tearing up over the baby's first heartbeat, or looking at grainy ultrasound pictures dissipated like the marine layer on a hot southern California day. She didn't know how she continued to get in the same situation over and over. Here she was again pregnant by a man she loved, who wanted her but not her baby. She had hoped that Nick's presence here meant that he had changed his mind about their future together, but she'd judged right from the beginning. She should have listened to reason and not been swayed by her sentimental side.

Maybe she had just confused lust with love. No couch equaled no responsibility. She'd known that all along. Before the doctor or nurse came back, she pulled her cell phone from her purse. It was time to enlist Sophie as her pregnancy coach. Nick was out of the picture, and she didn't intend to go through this alone.

Nick and his father were tackling the largest unpainted area of the house, the open plan living and dining rooms. There was

Impasse

little conversation between them, the only sound in the room consisted of the clank of ladders and the rhythmic swish of the paint rollers against the smooth plaster.

"Earth to Nicky," he heard his father say.

"Sorry, Dad. Did you ask me something? I've been a million miles away today."

"I could tell. What's on your mind? I don't think it has anything to do with painting—though you're doing a much better job than in the bedroom—so it's not lady trouble again, is it?"

Finishing two opposite walls, they both came down the ladders and started cleaning up, getting ready for a lunch break.

"Dad, I have something I need to tell you."

"Before lunch? Can't it wait until I get something in my belly? This painting has been hard work. These tall walls, climbing up and down the ladder—I don't even know if I should be doing this at my old age." He shook his head woefully. "So what are you gonna feed…"

"Holly's pregnant," Nick blurted unceremoniously then paused to let his father know he was serious. "You're going to be a grandfather."

Dominic's eyes lit up with joy then welled with tears. He wrapped Nick in a bear hug, lifting him off the ground.

"I knew it. I couldn't believe she'd made those delicious waffles and just ignored them. She looked just like Iris did when she was pregnant with you, glowing and beautiful, if not a little green around the gills." Dominic shook his head disbelievingly. "I'm finally going to be a grandfather. Well it's about time." His grin reached from ear to ear.

"What waffles?"

A sheepish smile crept over Dominic's lips. "When I was working on her closet, I may have mentioned that I skipped breakfast."

"Dad, you were supposed to be helping."

"I did help. Have you seen those closets? I did some beautiful work there. But let's get back to the topic at hand. So, Holly's pregnant with your little boy or girl. Are you happy?" he clapped his hands. "I, myself, couldn't be happier. When is she due? Are you getting married? It'll do my heart good to have a wedding and a birth in the coming year. Your mom would be thrilled, God rest her soul."

Nick was quiet, sealing and stacking the paint cans, and moving the ladders to lean against an unpainted wall.

Dominic continued even though Nick hadn't answered any of his questions. "So have you thought of names? And you still haven't answered me. Are you getting married?" Dominic held a hand to his heart, apologetic. "I know, I know, I'm old fashioned, but I still think it should be marriage before babies. But I'm flexible. It's the new millennium. Maybe babies can come before marriage nowadays."

Nick finally spoke when Dominic paused to take a breath.

"I'm not sure if we're going to be together."

"What? I'm confused." Dominic scratched his head exaggeratedly. "I thought you guys were going like gangbusters. You painted the bedroom just for her, despite what you say." When Nick shook his head, Dominic nodded his. "Plus, I haven't been able to reach you at night for weeks. She seems like a great girl. She's surely a great cook and pretty too. What gives?"

"It's not that I don't want to be with her, Dad. I really do. It's just that this baby thing came as a really big surprise. I was ready to explore a relationship between us—really get to know each other better—maybe move in together, I don't know. But I sure know that I'm not ready to be a father. I'm only twenty-six, Dad."

Dominic, only half-kidding, cuffed Nick on the head.

"So what did you say to her when she told you she was pregnant?"

"I don't think I really said anything."

Dominic winced. "How long ago did she tell you?"

"Maybe a couple of weeks."

"And you're just telling me now?" His voice rose an octave, his Chicago accent stronger and thicker by the minute.

"I'm just not prepared for this."

"I may be old, but the birds and the bees haven't changed since I was your age. She didn't get pregnant by herself. You better get prepared. What you're doing to Holly isn't right. Your mother and I didn't raise you this way."

"I need time," Nick said imploring his father to understand.

"Nick, time is not a luxury you have," Dominic said, exasperated. "Do you know what my greatest regret is? That I didn't stand up to your grandfather and marry your mother when we graduated from high school. Those years with her in Chicago and me out here were the hardest of my life.

"When she was diagnosed with that damned cancer, I regretted every single one of those days." Dominic drew out the last few words meaningfully. After a pause, he continued. "I was young and arrogant back then. If I had known that my days with your mother were numbered, I wouldn't have waited until she was at the altar to get up the courage to claim her as my own. If I can pass nothing else on to you, remember this: Don't make my same mistake."

Holly was flicking through her closet of form-fitting clothes, looking for something to wear that could fit comfortably around her expanding waist. If she had ever worked up the nerve to wear skinny jeans, that time had passed. The doorbell buzzed loudly. She made a vow then to ask her landlord if she could change the bell to something more pleasant if it was going to be pressed constantly. Tying her robe tight around what was becoming a bulge, Holly opened the door.

Even after the flurry of activity over the last few months, she wasn't expecting anyone, so it was a pleasant surprise to see a large bouquet of pink lilies coming through her door, followed by Dominic.

"Here, these are for you." Dominic thrust the flowers at her unceremoniously. Clearly, he was not a man who gave gifts to women often. The whole thing was as awkward as it was endearing.

"They were my Iris's favorite flower," he said. "I hope you like."

"What's the occasion?" Holly asked, inhaling the scent of the fragrant bouquet.

"Are you kidding? It's not every day I find out I'm going to be a grandfather." Dominic took her hand, kissing it gently. "You couldn't have made me any happier."

Busying herself getting a vase, filling it with water, then trimming the stems, and arranging the flowers just so, Holly avoided Dominic's eyes. "You've talked to Nick, then?"

He lowered his stout frame and sat heavily in Holly's kitchen chair. "He'll come around, Holly. I think this all took my Nicky a little by surprise."

"Can I be honest with you? I'm not asking you to take sides or anything… "

Dominic interrupted her, "There are no 'sides' where a new baby is concerned."

"I'm just a little… no, a lot surprised that Nick's pulled a disappearing act on me. For weeks, months, he's been trying to convince me we can be more than friends. And I'll admit, I was resistant for exactly this reason. I knew at some point our differences would come into the picture, though not quite like this. Dominic, I'm thirty-two and ready to settle down."

"Nicky wants all that. He's talked about it to me and his mom, God rest her soul. Of all my kids, I've always thought of him mostly as a family man. Lookit, he bought a house on his own before he got married. The others are all waiting to walk down the aisle before taking on a mortgage."

"That's all well and good, Dominic, but the minute he learned about my pregnancy, he pulled a Houdini. I felt like I had to twist his arm just to get him to the first prenatal appointment. That's not a good feeling, you know."

"I'm sorry, I didn't raise him this way," Dominic said, hanging his head shamefully. "I don't know what's come over him."

"I don't want my child to be unwanted," Holly said, feeling a twinge of the loneliness she felt as a child. "I have enough love for both of us."

"Even if Nicky doesn't come around, I'll be there as long as

I'm able. A child can never get too much love."

Tearing at Dominic's endearing promise, Holly could only nod.

"So are we having a boy or a girl? Do you have any names? Dominic is traditional in our family. You may want to consider it. I think it's a strong name for a boy."

"Is that Nick's real name? Is he a junior?" Holly asked momentarily flustered. It was embarrassing that she wasn't sure of the full name of the father of her child.

"No, my Iris didn't take to the whole junior business, so Nicholas was as close as I could get, but I think we could always use another Dominic in the family."

"I haven't really thought of names yet, but I don't want to know if it's a boy or girl until the birth."

"You want to be surprised, like we were in the old days?"

Holly nodded, warming to the topic. She and Dominic talked for more than an hour about babies, and family, and marriage. It was nice to not have to keep a secret and to have someone to share her enthusiasm.

"Truce?" Nick said into the phone without any introduction hours after Dominic had left.

"We're not at war, Nick," Holly said quietly. Then into the silence, broken by occasional static, Holly said, "Your dad came by today."

"I apologize if he intruded. He can be a bit overwhelming at times."

"There's nothing to be sorry for. He's a great guy." More silence.

Impasse

"I've been thinking that maybe we should go ahead with the Thanksgiving plans."

"You didn't call it off?"

"I didn't have the heart, Holly. I miss you. Can't we at least do this one thing together?"

"Does it change anything else between us?"

"I still need more time, Holly," he said quietly. She sighed, but didn't say anything else. She didn't ask all of the open-ended questions that came to her mind. The bottom line was that she missed him, too, desperately.

Against her better judgment, she agreed to help him put together the annual celebration.

Twelve

Holly maneuvered the car into Nick's garage, which he had thoughtfully left open. She still had her key to his house, but no opener for the garage. Holly had never thought to ask, and he had obviously never thought to give one. She popped the trunk, ready to pull out all the stuff she had bought for the dinner preparations. A fresh ten-pound turkey, and straight from the farmer's market, vegetables and fruits filled her car. Before she could load her arms up with bags for the trek upstairs, Nick bounded down the steps and nodded in greeting, averting his eyes from her scrutiny.

They didn't hug or kiss, and the loss of their earlier closeness left her bereft. Effortlessly, he picked up everything, leaving her with nothing more to carry than her purse.

Nick put almost everything away and organized the rest neatly on the granite counter, then looked at her, smiling and rubbing his hands together in anticipation. "So what's on the

Impasse

menu? What can I help you with?"

The kitchen, which had been comfortably cozy before, felt too intimate. Part of her, a large part actually, wanted to hug him, kiss him, ask that he hold her. The other part wanted to flee the unresolved mess they'd made of things. She did neither. Instead, Holly did the mature thing; she swallowed the lump in her throat and forged ahead.

"Well, of course we'll have turkey. I picked up a free range bird this morning from Harvey Guss, but we won't start that until tomorrow."

"Doesn't it need to defrost? My mom always left it out the day before."

Holly shook her head. "This one was never frozen—it tastes better that way. Anyway, today I'll start most of the other stuff." Holly gave Nick a rundown of what had to be done. They worked companionably in near silence for several hours, he cutting, dicing, and chopping. She put together the cornbread, sage, and sausage stuffing, prepared the candied sweet potatoes, apple, and pumpkin pies for dessert.

Nick cleared off the debris from the counter and looked at all the food ready to go into the ovens.

"The smell of all this great food is killing me. I'm absolutely starving. Want to stop for lunch?" Nick asked.

Holly suggested they go out. "If it's okay with you," she said, feeling tired and hungry all of a sudden. "I can't think about making a meal for us right now."

"Of course, you've been on your feet all morning. I'm certainly not in the mood for more cooking. Where would you like to go? I'll take you anywhere," he said, pulling his keys off the wall hook. The only decision they made before leaving the house was that they were going to wing it.

After they drove down the hill and hit Sunset Boulevard, Holly suggested that Nick head west. She wanted to go somewhere busy—nowhere that was remotely romantic to spark any deep or meaningful conversation. If he wasn't ready, she wasn't going to push. Holly pointed them to the Mitsuwa Marketplace, a Japanese food court that featured a ramen soup place that she loved. In addition to a good, filling lunch, the food court provided a loud and unsentimental atmosphere.

They sat, precariously balanced on small stools, their trays perched on the small bamboo topped counters that snaked through the food court. Twirling long, handmade noodles with their wooden chopsticks and slurping the rich tonkotsu broth left little time to talk about more than the niceties of when and how she'd discovered the market.

Nick was moving more slowly through his soup than Holly.

"Are you going to finish that?" Holly had finished her large bowl of shio ramen and the side dishes. Being pregnant and ravenous made her a lot less dainty. She certainly couldn't get by on a small salad and soup anymore.

"I have this voracious appetite right now," she explained a little apologetically. "I think I've gotten over the worst of the morning sickness, but I'm starving at meal times, and a lot of other times, too."

"How is … everything?" he asked, unable to meet her eyes.

"It's fine, Nick. Everything's fine. My second prenatal appointment went well. Everything seems to be progressing normally. Sophie's going to be my birth coach. I think she'll keep the class on its toes. I'm trying to find a class that specializes in single mothers—that way Sophie and I won't feel awkward."

Nick's face reddened. He looked everywhere but at her. Suddenly he was very busy fishing a small slice of pork from the bowl with his bamboo chopsticks.

"Have you told anyone at work?" he asked.

"I'll probably tell the VP of marketing in the next few weeks. I wanted to wait until I was at least three months along before I announced anything in case I lost… in case I had another miscarriage," Holly said, stumbling over the last few words.

"Anyway, I already have someone in mind who can step in as acting director when I'm gone. Plus, I'll be able to check in on the projects. Fortunately, this baby will come after the holiday rush. I like working during the holidays. This time of year, it's so much easier to find volunteers, so there are a bunch of projects we'll do in December.

"Don't work too hard," he admonished.

"Oh, Nick, don't worry, I'm listening to my body and taking care of myself." Just then, Holly started yawning and couldn't stop. She felt suddenly exhausted, emotionally and physically. It was hard pretending everything was okay when she was terrified of starting her son or daughter's life as a single mom. Tiredness swept over Holly like a tidal wave. Through her hand, which she was using to try to stifle her next yawn, she asked, "Do you mind taking me home? I'm really tired, and don't think I can stay awake all the way back to your place, then drive myself home. I'll have someone drive me to pick up my car later."

"Of course, Holly, no problem." Nick jumped up, busing their table before gently helping her up. He kept a supportive arm around her waist as they walked to the car then helped her in, buckling her into place. She couldn't keep her eyes open no matter how hard she tried.

She came awake when she heard her name called.

"We're here," he said.

"I'm sorry about that. I must be more exhausted than I thought. I seem to fall asleep anywhere and everywhere nowadays. The doctor said it should pass in the next couple of weeks as my body adjusts," Holly said. Soon, she became cognizant of her surroundings, aware that she was back at Nick's. "You should have taken me to my home, Nick."

"Shhh," Nick said, gently pulling her from the car. "Let me help you in."

"I'm okay, I can get to my car and drive myself home under my own steam," Holly said pulling against Nick, even though she was more firmly planted in his car.

"Holly, let me help you," Nick objected. "You just said you're in no condition to drive yourself home. Please let me do this one thing for you."

If she hadn't been so tired, Holly would have fought this renewed sense of intimacy between them, but she couldn't muster up the energy to protest. So she let Nick help her up the stairs and into his bedroom. She fell asleep almost instantly.

Nick undressed the sleeping Holly, caressing her body with his eyes. Changes which would probably be imperceptible to others amazed him. Her breasts which were just a little fuller than before were lined with smallish, blue veins. Her abdomen had gone from concave to just slightly convex. The slight muscle definition she'd developed from yoga had softened.

When he had put her clothes in the one chair in the room, he lay next to her watching her deep even breathing, her breasts rising and falling with each breath, loving her so much his heart ached, but not liking himself very much for letting her down when she obviously needed him the most.

As dusk shadowed the bedroom, Holly awoke to find Nick watching her. She couldn't tell how long she'd slept tucked warmly in Nick's sleigh bed. He must have undressed her because she was nude under the feather duvet and blanket. The soft sheets brushed against her suddenly sensitive skin, her hardened nipples. Holly spotted her clothes neatly folded on a new, comfortable looking leather chair she hadn't seen before. She reached out her arm to pull back the covers and grab her clothes, but Nick stopped her with a hungry glance.

"Nick, what are you doing?" she said, somewhat resigned to their unshakeable desire for each other. "What are we doing?"

"What we do best," he said huskily. "Making each other feel good."

Before she could protest, Nick laid a finger upon her lips, still puffy from sleep. From that moment forward their communication was strictly non-verbal. They looked intently in each other's eyes. While Nick stroked her hair, face, then her arm, raising goose bumps along the sensitive flesh, she was unable to tear her eyes away from his. She watched his incredibly vivid green eyes turn as dark as night with desire.

Against her better judgment, Holly gave in to the feelings he aroused in her so easily. She surrendered to Nick, erasing the weeks of loneliness and pent up emotions overwhelming her. Nick eased her leg over his hip, his hand dipping to her core, testing her readiness. Needing no further invitation, he guided his shaft, entering her slowly yet deliberately, letting her soft warmth envelop him. With no barriers between them, they sighed in pleasure when they came together. Holly and Nick stayed joined like that for a long stretch of time, only the slightest rocking keeping them moving together in a rhythm they alone had perfected.

They remained on the knife's edge of pleasure for what seemed like forever until Holly couldn't take it anymore. She leaned into him and kissed him in that way she knew he couldn't resist, caressing his bottom lip with her tongue. His breath caught and their slow rhythm broke, his strokes becoming faster, deeper, erratic, and barely controlled. He broke the kiss and reached between them to gently tweak each of her beaded nipples before stroking the pad of his thumb along her clitoris until she pulsed around him, her climax milking him until he reached his own.

They lay joined and not moving as the sky darkened from dusk into night. He slowly disentangled himself and went down the hallway to the bathroom. When he came back, Holly was almost fully dressed and slipped on her sandals, her painted toenails peeking out.

"Where are you going now?"

"Home, Nick."

"But… " he trailed off, his eyes on the very rumpled bedclothes.

"What just happened wasn't a very good idea."

"But I love you, Holly."

"I know Nick; I love you, too," she said softly, her declaration barely audible in the dark room. She had finally admitted to him what she had only reluctantly admitted to herself. Holly paused, her confession standing between them like an unwanted guest in the room. She wanted to ask if that love extended to their son or daughter growing inside her, but she could not bear to hear the answer. She dreaded hearing that he did not want them both.

"What just happened doesn't change anything," she continued. "I've already lived this lesson, Nick, and I'm not going down this road again. I know now that sometimes love isn't enough."

On Thanksgiving Day, Holly came back at seven o'clock in the morning as she had promised, carrying a few more items in a large multi-colored tote. Nick was subdued, trying his best not to upset her. He hoisted the turkey into the oven when she asked and did all of the other heavy lifting required. He watched her set the table with beautiful things from her stash of family heirlooms.

Sophie was first to arrive that afternoon, reluctantly admitting that Ryan was with her. "He tagged along," she whispered out of Ryan's earshot. But the smoldering looks that passed between them once or twice belied Sophie's blasé attitude.

Asha and Hayes came next. Hayes, bartender guide in hand, immediately set himself up in the kitchen making hot buttered rum for everyone. Asha curled her long legs on the living room floor, and for her normally soft-spoken demeanor, revealed a surprisingly loud voice as she cheered on the Detroit Lions. When asked, Asha admitted in her mellifluous accent that she had never been to Michigan. Helena came with a few of Nick's friends from the studio and network. Last to arrive was Dominic, who carried something sealed in a large padded container looking like he had a pizza to deliver.

"Dad, what took you so long? We've been holding dinner for you."

"I was busy, Nicky. You're not the only one with important stuff do."

"What could be important today? You knew we were having dinner. Why didn't you answer your phone?" Nick asked, pointing to the slim mobile hanging from Dominic's belt.

"I don't need that newfangled gadget you bought me. I was out doing something very critical we'll talk about later. Now let's stop being rude to your guests, and get down to the chow."

He batted away anyone who offered to help him with the mystery package, saying only that he had something special for later. Holly eyed Nick warily, and he just shrugged, going along for the ride. He was used to Dominic's eccentricities.

As Nick had remembered from years past, Holly's food was a hit. Everyone wanted to know how she kept the turkey moist and what she did to make everything taste so great. Like any good chef, she did not reveal too many of her secrets. Not to denigrate his mom's memory, but they always had leftovers after Thanksgiving even in his large family. This was not the case with Holly's dinner. Just as quickly as the feast seemed to appear, it was gone. Regrettably, he wouldn't be eating turkey sandwiches or leftover pumpkin pie.

Sated, the guys were talking about moving to the living room to watch the second football game of the day. Holly and Helena

Impasse

were comparing recipes, and Nick felt content. He was where he wanted to be, surrounded by the woman he loved, his family, and his friends.

That feeling of contentment slowly started to disintegrate when Dominic started unzipping his mystery container. Before anyone had made a move from the table, Dominic was passing around crystal flutes, and pulling out bottles of chilled champagne and sparkling grape juice. It was like watching, in slow motion, a collision he knew was going to take place but was powerless to stop.

Holly gazed at Nick wide-eyed with trepidation. He could only give the faintest of shrugs and an almost imperceptible shake of his head. He knew once his dad had set his mind to something, it was best to let things run their course.

Dominic halted the conversation with a clink of his teaspoon on his flute. "I have an important announcement." With that declaration, all conversation died down. "Thank you all for being here today. It's good to have both old friends and new friends around during the holidays." There were a few nods of assent, and a couple of people clinked glasses.

"I'm fortunate this year that I'm able to spend Thanksgiving with one of my children, and with Holly who I've come to think of as family." A tear escaped Dominic's eye as he continued. "You'll have to excuse me, I get a little emotional," he said, wiping the drop from his face with the handkerchief he always carried, a throwback to an earlier era. "I suspected I wouldn't be able to last through a whole speech because I'm so proud I feel like I'm going to burst." He paused again to gather himself.

"I would like to propose a toast, to Holly and Nick, and my

new grandson or granddaughter we'll soon welcome into this world."

There was a pause as Dominic's meaning became clear to everyone. Then a great cacophony of sound erupted as everyone clinked glasses with each other and issued good tidings to Nick and Holly. Asha winked at Holly and said in her breathy, accented English, "I knew you must have been cooking up something. We haven't seen you much at all in the last few months."

Hayes finished the thought, "I think she was getting a bun in the oven." Everyone laughed. Holly only nodded, dipping her head to sip the sparkling juice.

"When are you due?" Helena asked.

"The last week of May," she answered quietly.

"Are you coming to New York then, to have the baby?" someone else asked.

"Right," one of Nick's studio mates, an Australian named Jack, chimed in. "We'll be working on the new film next spring."

Nick stole a sidelong glance at Holly. "We haven't decided how we're going to do that part yet. The timing was a little unexpected."

Another of Nick's studio friends, a serious looking young blond, piped in next. "So when are you two getting married?"

With every question, Nick wondered where Holly's breaking point was. They'd just found it. "Alison, we're not getting married, not now, probably not ever," she said even more softly, abruptly ending the discussion. "Now can someone help with these dishes?" After an uncomfortably long silence, there was no shortage of hands to help her clean up. With everyone chipping in, the table was cleared and the dishwasher loaded in no time.

Impasse

Dominic even volunteered to put out the garbage, though he cursed the narrow stairs all the way down.

Holly was sitting quietly in the dining area sipping tea while everyone else congregated in the living room around the football game when Sophie decided to join her. "That was some show Dominic put on," Sophie said, raising her eyebrows.

"Yeah, it was," Holly said resignedly.

"Have things changed?" Sophie asked, her gray eyes eagerly searching Holly's face for some sign.

"No," Holly said, trying to keep the tears from her eyes and the quaver from her voice. "I think Dominic's just hopeful. I finally told Nick yesterday that I love him, and it didn't make a difference." She swiped at a tear escaping her eyes, determined not to cry. "He's been pushing all along to 'be a couple,' and 'have a relationship.' But I don't think he can expand his definition of 'us' to include our child," she said, bracketing us in air quotes with her hand.

"What are you going to do now? Are you going to New York when he works on that film?"

"I can't, and I'm not sure I want to. I can't really afford to quit my job now or take any kind of extended leave. If I combine my inheritance with the money from the property sale, I can just afford a little house somewhere like Silver Lake. Maybe take some time off after the baby is born… play it by ear from there."

Sophie's face looked as sad as Holly felt. "I'm so sorry, I thought it would work out, especially when I saw you guys today. You looked and acted so much like a couple."

Holly sniffled and wiped her nose, more determined than

ever not to cry. She was done crying. It was time to act.

With a watery smile, Holly playfully poked Sophie in the side. "Speaking of looking like a couple, what's going on with you and Ryan?" Sophie turned as red as her hair used to be.

"Nothing, really," she said. "We're exact opposites, but something about him gets to me."

They talked for a long time, Holly excited over the new life growing inside her. The burgeoning love for her baby was helping her deal with the waning disappointment over the way she and Nick were ending things. As the game wrapped up, their friends said their goodbyes. Ryan was lingering at the door looking like he would do anything to get Sophie alone. Sophie pulled Holly aside as Dominic and Nick straightened up the downstairs rooms.

"Are you going to be okay?"

"It's fine. I'm going to leave in a little bit. Don't worry about me. I think Nick and I have made our peace with where we are. If I were you, I'd be worried about that man over there, who looks like he wants to devour you for dessert."

Sophie gave her a swift hug then rushed from Nick's place in her usual whirlwind fashion. Ryan trailed behind in her wake, a little dazed, looking like he was going along for the ride but certainly enjoying it.

Ignoring the Andreis men's protests, Holly put away the clean dishes, still warm from the dishwasher, and scoured the pots and pans.

While she was drying, she looked from her lover to his father sitting at the table, both at a loss for words.

"Well, happy Thanksgiving, you guys."

Impasse

"Are you leaving?" Nick asked. His eyes pleaded with her for mercy.

"Nick, I think we shouldn't see each other right now."

Dominic stood abruptly, causing one of the dining room chairs to wobble slightly. "I can take a hint. Now seems like a good time to measure the back patio for those Saltillo tiles you wanted, Nicky."

Nick's father went outside without a tape measure.

"I know you're not happy with me right now, but please don't be mad at my Dad. He was just—"

Holly interrupted. "Don't even think about it. I could never really be angry with Dominic. He was just doing what came naturally. He's a sweet man, and I know he'll make a wonderful grandfather."

"Are you really going home tonight?"

"I have to, Nick. Our relationship is too stressful. And stress is the last thing I need right now."

Nick looked like he wanted to say something but couldn't get the words out. She shook her head, gathered her purse, and let herself out.

Dominic appeared by Nick's side in the time it took him to blink. He would never accuse his father of eavesdropping, but it seemed like he'd come back into the house awfully quick.

"So what about those tiles?"

"I don't give a damn about any ceramic tiles, Nicky. Why did you let her leave?"

"She wanted to go home," Nick said, resigned.

"Don't get smart with me. You know what I'm asking

you. Why aren't you two together, getting married, or at least committing to… I don't know… something?"

Nick winced at his father's characterization. "I'm not sure about anything right now."

"Not sure. Just a few weeks ago, you were singing her praises. I couldn't even get you on your cell phone. What the heck changed?"

"She's having a baby."

"You keep saying that. Am I misunderstanding the birds and the bees? Maybe we need to have this talk again. Maybe you didn't hear so good when you were thirteen."

"I know, Dad, I know. She's having our baby. Fatherhood's a huge responsibility—a lifelong commitment. I just don't think I'm ready for that."

"What do you mean you're not ready for that? You were certainly ready to have her as a girlfriend. The way you were renovating the house at the speed of light, I thought you were going to ask her to move in. Do you think relationships are only about the lust in the beginning?"

"Dad," Nick said, embarrassed to have his father talking or even thinking about his sex life. "I just don't think I'm ready to be a father now. Will I still be able to pursue my filmmaking or will I have to take some 'Joe job' and compromise my vision? And what if, maybe, I'm not done sowing my oats?" Nick paused a long time. "What if she isn't the 'one'?"

"Nicky, if you hear nothing else I say, please hear this. You have something here worth saving, and the longer you take to make a decision, the less likely Holly will take you back." He paused, looking hard at his son. "Don't be immature or naïve

Impasse

about this. Do you know what commitment phobic men discover after ten, twenty years of searching?"

Nick shook his head.

"There is no there there. What you have is rare and special. Don't throw it away for some unknown dream. She's not asking you to give up anything. But if you leave her, you'll lose everything."

Thirteen

Sharp pains pierced the fuzzy halo of sleep that surrounded Holly. She sat up abruptly. The duvet pooled around her waist causing goose bumps to rise along her arms. For a moment the pain subsided and Holly, half asleep, lay her head down again, trying to warm up, thinking she had imagined it all. When the second pain came, however, she knew it was for real. Holly looked at the clock. It was three in the morning.

Her heart beat a rapid tattoo as she tried to talk herself down from a full-on panic attack. She tried to convince herself she couldn't be having a second miscarriage. It was probably some kind of false labor. Holly refused to allow anything bad to happen to her baby. Everything would be okay. It had to be. The third jagged pain and the appearance of bright red blood on her sheets told her it was all too real.

She pulled herself up from the bed, no longer caring about the chill in the room, and retrieved the cordless phone receiver from the kitchen wall. Since agreeing to be her birth coach, Sophie was number one on the speed dial. She pressed the number that corresponded with Sophie's cell phone and listened to the monotonous rings, hoping her friend answered the phone before the call went to voice mail. A groggy Sophie croaked a greeting into the phone.

"I think it's happening again. I'm losing the baby," Holly said on the edge of hysteria.

There was a clunk as Sophie dropped, then retrieved the phone.

"Okay, don't panic. Call nine-one-one and I'll meet you at the hospital. Tell them your doctor is at Cedars and they should take you there."

Holly disconnected and gave her particulars to the nine-one-one operator who answered her next frantic call. The ten-minute wait for the city's paramedics were the longest minutes of her life. Her normally quiet street blazed with light and sirens as a small fire truck and ambulance came screaming down the block.

The ride to the hospital was a blur. Holly tried the best she could to answer the questions the medics put to her, but the overwhelming fear and dread made it difficult to concentrate on their inquiries. Fortunately, Sophie was already at the waiting room answering the numerous questions. She stayed close by as they wheeled Holly to a semi-private curtained area.

A resident did a quick pelvic exam then brought in the obstetrician on call. They had an animated, whispered conference before the taller of the two spoke with her.

"Holly Prentice?" When she nodded, he made the introductions before addressing her case. "We've done a preliminary exam."

Holly couldn't wait for the niceties. "Am I going to lose my baby?"

They shook their heads. "No, ma'am, you're not going to miscarry. What I think we've got here is cervical insufficiency. In layman's terms it's an incompetent uterus."

"What in the heck does that mean—in real English?" Sophie asked in her newly self-appointed role as Holly's advocate.

The doctor looked away from them and down at the pager buzzing persistently on his belt. "I'll let your regular doctor explain it to you. He should be here in the next twenty minutes or so. But with surgery and bed rest, you should deliver a healthy, full-term baby." And then he left the semi-secluded area as quickly as he had entered.

Holly turned a worried gaze toward Sophie, the word surgery reverberating through her head. Without uttering a sound, Sophie grabbed her hand and they sat that way, silently, until Dr. Cole came into the bay.

A little calmer than when she came in, the light sedatives they gave her taking effect, Holly introduced Sophie to Dr. Cole as her birth coach and best friend. Thankfully, he was kind enough not to ask about Nick.

"Holly, I'm not sure what the previous doctors explained, but let me assure you that you will deliver your baby if I have anything to say about it."

Holly visibly relaxed, and Sophie breathed a sigh of relief, briskly rubbing the color back into Holly's ice-cold hands.

"You appear to have a weak cervix. The weight of your growing baby could cause your cervix to open unexpectedly. This may

Impasse

have been the cause of your earlier miscarriage, or alternatively, the subsequent D&C after you miscarried could have caused this problem." He shrugged a little uncertainly. "Either way, we may never know. The bottom line is that your rapidly growing fetus put pressure on your cervix, and that's what caused tonight's false labor pains and spotting."

"Can you fix it?" Holly asked softly, her very breath depending on the answer Dr. Cole gave. "The first doctor mentioned something about surgery?"

"We will have to do surgery to protect your baby," Dr. Cole said gravely. "I would perform a procedure called cervical cerclage—basically stitching the cervix closed so that the baby stays inside where he or she belongs."

"What's the downside?" she asked, knowing that saving her baby would not come without a cost.

"You will have to be on complete bed rest for the next few weeks and possibly the remainder of your pregnancy, and sexual activity is strictly forbidden."

Holly didn't even blink. "I'll do anything to save my baby."

The doctor paused and looked at Holly, then Sophie a little uneasily.

"I don't want to tread on anyone's toes here, but would you like to call the baby's father, include him on this decision?"

Sophie nodded, but Holly shook her head vigorously. "There is no need for that. We're not together anymore. I'll be making all the decisions," Holly said, her tone brooking no argument. Sophie leaned down to Holly's ear, her body blocking the doctor's view, giving them a small modicum of privacy.

"I think we should call Nick. This decision is going to affect him, too, you know."

"How?" Holly whispered back just as fiercely. "He wasn't exactly dying to be a part of this process. I haven't talked to him in two weeks, and I don't see that changing anytime soon. Do you?"

A semi-private hospital room was all her health insurance would spring for, but mercifully the other bed was empty. Holly could finally relax knowing the surgery was scheduled for the next day. Sophie had cranked up the head and footrest and was resting in the bed's contorted V, pretending it was comfortable in an effort to make Holly laugh. The two settled in, talking and laughing, and for a while it seemed like one big sleep-over party—albeit in a room lit like a morgue.

When the wide faux wooden door swung open for what seemed like the thousandth time, she was sure it was yet another nurse coming to take her blood pressure or temperature or to check on her cervix. She was just about to comment to Sophie on the utter lack of privacy in hospitals when she glanced at the lone, tall figure that had come into the room. Her heartbeat escalated, causing the monitor to beep erratically and betray her feelings. She was embarrassed that he could still cause such a reaction. Holly felt like the bottom had dropped out of her stomach, out of her world.

"Nick," she sputtered. "What are you doing here… how did you… know?" Then it dawned on her: Sophie. Her best friend had flattened the bed and was just about to surreptitiously take her leave when Holly's voice slowed her. "Did you call him?" She felt betrayed. She didn't want Nick hanging around because of his sense of guilt or obligation. He had to know that she was more than capable of handling things on her own.

"I'm here because I love you," he said simply.

Holly had no quip, no crafty response to Nick's words. His simple declaration unarmed her. After weeks of building up an emotionally impenetrable wall, she was vulnerable to him all over again.

Dr. Cole chose that moment to check on Holly during his last rounds. At Nick's request, he again explained how Holly's cervix was too weak to hold the baby in, and that a few well-placed stitches would prevent early labor or a second trimester miscarriage. "I just want to reiterate to you what I warned Holly about earlier. For the next few weeks, and possibly for the duration of the pregnancy, she'll need to be on bed rest," Dr. Cole admonished. "The two of you will need to follow my orders very strictly." Nick didn't blink or look put out by the fact that they would be prohibited from engaging in sexual intercourse.

Sophie went home to rest, shower, and change. The nurses rolled in a cot for Nick that fit next to her bed, but rather than talk, he just held her hand and stroked her hair until she slept. She woke a couple of times during her second night in the hospital when the nurses checked on her, and Nick never moved from her side. Though she was loathe to admit it, having Nick there made the experience a lot less scary. With him by her side, she could get through almost anything.

Holly was prepared for the epidural early the next morning. She only had to grit her teeth a little to get through the first sharp sting of pain while they inserted the needle. Then she was wheeled away to surgery alone. Before the orderly pushed her gurney away, Nick promised he would be there when she got back. The procedure was surprisingly quick. Holly was back in her bed in little more than an hour. When she was wheeled back in to the room, a small group awaited her. Sophie had returned, and somewhere along the way Dominic had come as well.

Holly's voice was a little hoarse when she spoke. "What are you guys all doing here? It was just a little surgery."

Dominic was the first to answer. "We're family, and that's what family does. I'm here for you, Holly, for the good and bad." Then he mumbled something under his breath that sounded like "I can't say the same for my son." But Holly wasn't sure she heard right and didn't want to press the issue. Even if they had no real holds on each other, she was glad Nick was here, too. She was no longer ashamed to admit that she needed to lean on someone right now.

Dominic continued, "So I hear you're on bed rest starting today."

Holly nodded. "I think for a little while. At least until the doctor is sure that the surgery takes, and there won't be any further complications with the baby."

"Where are you going to stay?" Dominic asked with concern in his voice.

Holly hadn't given much thought to the question. "Home. My place. It's only for a short while, I think. Between Sophie and my other girlfriends, I'll be fine."

"The studio's production schedule is slowing down as people gear up for the holiday season. I'm sure I can stop by to check on you during our breaks… " Sophie trailed off.

Impasse

"You're coming home with me. No arguments," Nick interrupted the back and forth between the women.

"Nick, I can't inconvenience you that way."

"Look, I'm wrapping up the last film and doing pre-production on the New York project. I can work just as well from home as I can from the studio."

Holly didn't think her heart could stand it—loving him, but not being able to have him. She was trying to come up with a clever way to extricate herself when a nurse they hadn't met before picked that opportune time to enter the room. A sheaf of multicolored pages filled her hands.

"I'm your discharge nurse," she said. "I have some postoperative procedures to review with you."

She explained how the sutures would heal and the symptoms of possible complications worth calling the doctor about. Sophie and Dominic were joking softly about something while the nurse talked. Then she got to the part about bed rest.

The woman silenced them all with one look. "Now, as the mother's support system, it's important for all of you to understand the importance of bed rest. At this stage of the pregnancy it's critical, and it will end when the doctor decides it's safe for the mom to return to limited or normal activity, okay?"

Everyone nodded, mollified.

"Here are the dos and don'ts," she said, handing Holly a pink sheet. "You are going to have to recline or lie down twenty-four hours a day. You can get up to use the bathroom and to shower once a day. That's it. No dishes. No laundry. And most importantly, no sex. There will be no other activity. I want to be crystal clear about this. It's like taking penicillin. You have to follow the whole course; there can be no halfway with this. If you ever have any questions about what you can do—stay in bed—and what you can't do—anything else—please call Dr. Cole's office." She handed over another page, this one turquoise, and left the room on the turn of her crepe-soled heel.

The seriousness of the instructions cast a somber mood about the room.

"This is all the more reason that you should be with me," Nick said in a way that brooked no argument.

Neither Sophie nor Dominic looked like they were willing to challenge him. Against her better judgment, Holly capitulated.

"Okay, I'll go to Nick's. But I'm going to need some stuff."

"Where's your purse?" Nick pointed to his father and Sophie. "You two. Go get her stuff."

He pulled her key ring from the bag and handed the jumble of metal to Sophie and Dominic.

While she made a quick list of the things she would need on a small pad the hospital had provided in the bedside table, Nick started making more calls to arrange for Holly's convalescence. Sophie and Dominic took off to put her stuff together. Other than having Holly sign some papers, Nick handled the rest of the check-out process.

He wheeled her through the lobby and to his car. A valet had pulled the car to the entrance.

"For now, we're doing this my way," Nick said.

Fourteen

Nick's grasp was firm as he gently helped her up the stairs and then carried her to the bedroom, holding her as if she was precious, breakable crystal. She tried not to think about another time when a man would carry her over the threshold. Before she could get herself situated in the king-size sleigh bed, she heard the front door open, and Sophie and Dominic bustled in.

They were upstairs in a flash with her small suitcase and a couple of shopping bags full of various and sundry items. Following Nick's cues, Sophie put Holly's clothes in the half-empty armoire, while Dominic stacked her toiletries on the dresser. Then Nick and his father disappeared to get something, though she couldn't remember requesting anything else. About fifteen minutes later, they had a small TV with a built-in DVD player set up in the corner of the room. Dominic had brought the electronics from his own bedroom.

Holly was touched. "I don't know how to thank you."

"Just keep my first grandchild safe and healthy," Dominic said. They stayed a few more minutes to make sure she was comfortable. Then she and Nick were truly alone. Even though she was carrying the man's child, and they had shared intimacies far greater than sharing a room, Holly felt as awkward as she did that first night she'd been alone with him in this house.

"You don't—" Holly started.

"Are you—" Nick said at the same time, their words crashing into each other.

"You first," she said.

"I was going to ask you if you were hungry or needed anything."

"No, Nick, I'm fine. I was just going to take a little nap if that's okay. I didn't get much sleep at the hospital with all the bright lights and nurses walking in and out of the room at all hours of the night."

"If you're okay, I'm going to go up to the loft and get myself set up to work at home. I just want to see if I need anything from the studio while I'm working here."

"Go ahead. Don't worry about me," Holly said, yawning sleepily. She turned on her side and buried her head in the fluffy pillow. She heard Nick go up to the loft, and though she was exhausted, she could not doze off. Their future, if any, weighed heavily on her mind. Just two days ago, she was ready to move past the idea of them being together, having a "forever." But hope was burgeoning again. Something seemed to have shifted in Nick. She couldn't put her finger on it exactly, but something was there.

Above her in the nook that comprised the third floor loft, she heard Nick power up his iMac and slide in a DVD of the last edit of Solstice's documentary. When the voices of the Esperanza kids came to life, he hit the mute button.

"Nick," Holly called up. "There's no need to turn it down. I'm not sleeping anyway. This is why I didn't want to be here. I am not going to disturb your work or your life. Please turn it back up. I'd like to feel like I'm a part of things, not some Victorian invalid closed up in a room."

His muffled chuckle was barely audible.

Holly must have eventually drifted off because she was startled when Nick woke her up in time for dinner. They shared a simple meal. He had wine and she, water. Then he helped her to the bathroom for a quick shower. "I think I'm going to turn in," she said.

He looked at the clock. "Then I'll come to bed, too."

"You're going to sleep here?"

"We're adults, Holly. I can control my libido around you, and I only have the one bed."

"Mm hm," Holly nodded, getting comfortable. He got under the covers, but his presence did nothing to bridge the impossible gulf between them.

"Plus, I'll be here if anything happens."

Holly tossed and turned for nearly an hour. Sleep eluded her again, even though she was still deathly tired.

Nick came closer, laying his head on her pillow. "You still awake?"

"I can't get to sleep. Maybe it's because of the strange bed."

"You never had a problem sleeping here before. What's really bothering you?"

Holly tried unsuccessfully to hide the quaver in her voice. "I'm scared, Nick. I'm afraid of losing this baby."

He pulled her into his arms, his front to her back. He whispered into her sweetly scented hair, "Tell me about the last time."

"I don't really want to talk about it."

"Let me share some of this burden with you."

Hesitantly, she started talking. "Drew and I were fighting all the time. I had wanted a baby for years, and he felt that the pregnancy had trapped him." Holly stopped to take a choppy breath, the memories assailing her now. "I kept trying to convince him that a baby was a blessing, but I wasn't getting through. All he could see was how a little boy or girl was going to stunt his career, his social life, the neat little world he'd built for himself."

Holly paused while Nick rubbed her back. "I was just so exhausted with the pregnancy, with the fighting, and that night, I was trying to relax. We had just gone to bed when I suddenly had these horrible cramps. It was so much worse than any period I'd ever had. Then the blood came. That was the scariest part. I knew then that the baby had died. Going to the hospital, the subsequent procedure, all of that was anticlimactic. It was that one dreadful moment I realized I wouldn't be a mother that I died a little inside."

Nick squeezed her. "My God, it must have been like déjà vu the other night."

Holly just nodded, and with that burden lifted off her, and Nick's gentle back rub, she drifted off to sleep at last.

Impasse

A cool fall morning light crept into the room and Holly stirred, the cacophony of coyote yelps and sharp barks bringing her to wakefulness. Nick had his back to her, but when she pulled up the covers, he turned over to face her.

"Did you hear that?" she whispered, her eyes growing wide as the canines' voices merged into one long, feral song.

"It's just a couple of coyotes howling to each other."

"A couple," Holly said. "It sounds like so many. People who live in the hills are always telling stories about them living in the Santa Monica Mountains, but I didn't think they'd live so close," she said, shivering a little at the sound. "Do you ever see them?"

"Sometimes when I'm coming home late at night, I see them darting across the road. Their eyes glow in the car's headlights, kind of like dogs."

"Are they dangerous?" Holly asked, thinking about the children she'd seen running freely in the neighborhood.

"Nah, they're okay," Nick said, sounding unconcerned. "They're much smaller than they sound. I know they hunt small animals like squirrels and the like, but they tend to stay away from humans."

Though assured by Nick's knowledge, Holly trembled as the coyotes continued to yowl. Sensing her fright, Nick pulled her into his arms. She went willingly. It was comforting to be held by this man she loved, despite the emotional gulf between them. When she was in his embrace, all of her problems, and much of the uncertainty surrounding their relationship, melted away. The coyote yips and barks died down as the sky lightened. The usual array of morning birdcalls filled the cool morning air, taking over where the coyotes had left off.

Holly didn't notice at first that Nick had shifted a little. Though one arm was looped lightly around her waist, the other was lightly stroking her silky curls and her back. She started having that familiar warm and tingly feeling reserved for Nick's touch. When he leaned in to stroke her lips lightly with his, Holly ignored the little voice in her mind that told her they were treading on very treacherous ground. Since they'd both heard the doctor's admonishment, she wanted to believe they wouldn't go too far.

Nick tried to remain aware of her medically prescribed boundaries. For right now, just kissing Holly's lips, full and pouty with sleep, and caressing her sleep-warmed body under the down-filled duvet was enough. Before Holly had waltzed back into his life the night of the housewarming party, he had been celibate for nearly a year, so a few months of abstinence would be no sweat.

He was proud of his restraint until he lowered his hands further and brushed them past her hips and toward her inner thighs, slick with the evidence of her desire. Suddenly, the wall he thought he had carefully erected between them crumbled. His body was on overdrive—and more than anything, he wanted to sheath himself in her and slake his savage hunger. Sensing the change between them, Holly was the first to pull away.

"Nick, the doctor's orders..." she said haltingly, her breathing nearly as rapid as his.

Nick took a deep, shuddering breath trying to calm his thudding heart. "I know I can't be deep inside you, but I'd like to pleasure you in other ways. It makes me feel good to make you come," Nick said stroking her again. His penis grew still harder between them, nudging against her thighs as if by design.

Holly scooted farther toward the edge of the king-size bed. Nick's hand fell away from her. "I think we've got our wires crossed here. The doctor was more explicit with me than with you I guess. It's not just sex that's prohibited, Nick; I can't have an orgasm either. The intensity of the spasms could cause problems for my baby as well."

Nick sighed as the enormity of what she said rolled over him. He felt Holly tentatively reach out and grasp his cock. "I think I can… "

"No, Holly, please don't," Nick said hoarsely, pushing her hand away and getting out of bed abruptly. "I'm sorry, I just need to cool off for a minute," he said and stalked from the room.

Holly suddenly felt defeated. The warmth and desire cooled abruptly. She noticed the pressure on her bladder and was glad to get out of bed for one of the three or four trips allowed that day. The light was on in the bathroom, and Holly felt comforted by the fact Nick had left it on for her. She was wholly unprepared for the sight that awaited her. Nick's outstretched arm braced his nude body against the moss green tile wall of the shower while the other hand moved slowly and deliberately on his erection. Her gasp caught Nick's attention.

"I'm sorry," Nick said, his movements stilling.

"No, it's okay," she said, "I understand." Her face grew as warm as his, and she was certain as red. Holly almost tripped on her bathrobe's belt backing out of the room.

On the one hand, she was extremely aroused by the idea that

she could get Nick so hot and bothered, so turned on. On the other, she was overwhelmed with the sacrifice he would have to make over the next few months if they stayed together like this. She could see no better reason for him to turn to a younger, healthier woman to fulfill his obvious needs. Falling back on the pillows in the oversized bed, Holly felt old and neutered. One of the last connections she and Nick had left was gone.

Holly heard the shower taps squeak to a halt a couple of minutes before Nick came back in the room. As embarrassed as she felt, she would have liked nothing more than for the mattress to swallow her whole.

Nick lay on the other side of the bed, the chasm between them as big as the Pacific Ocean.

Holly waded into the silence. "Are we okay?"

Nick reached over and pulled her into his arms. "We're more than okay," he said, stroking her hair. "Always."

"It's just that… I can't imagine what this is like for you," Holly said miserably. "I can go home if that will be easier."

"I'll be honest. It'll be hard. No pun intended," Nick said, chuckling against her hair. "Seriously, I won't deny it. I get hard thinking about you in my bed, thinking about you naked, thinking about making love with you." Nick pulled Holly's hand toward his boxer briefs. She instinctively curled her hand around his semi-hard penis. "And that's after taking matters into my own hands, so to speak," he said hoarsely, pulling her hand away from his. "That doesn't mean that I can't or wouldn't be able to control myself around you." Nick patted her slightly protruding abdomen. "This baby is too important for that."

Fifteen

After the first few awkward days, they fell into a routine. She would shower in the morning, then they'd watch a movie over breakfast, alternating between her choice and his. Then he went to the studio or worked at home in the afternoons while she read. What started as a fun vacation turned into days of boredom. She couldn't imagine how she would make it a few more weeks or months on bed rest. She put in a call to her boss. There had to be a way she could balance her work life and having this baby.

Holly closed her cell phone after the quick conversation. Nick was in the loft, editing. She hated bothering him, but she summoned him after thinking about a month more in bed.

"Nick," she called. "Can I ask you for a favor?"

He came down immediately, his worn jeans pulling tight across his cute little butt.

"I was just talking to my boss. I think I'm going to try to work a little while I'm on bed rest. I'll have Sophie bring over my laptop today."

"Do you think that's such a good idea?"

"I'm going to need to do something, Nick. I'm going out of my mind here."

"What's wrong with the way it's been going?"

"I can't pay my rent by watching movies with you in the morning and reading or napping the afternoon away, Nick." She paused, getting her temper under control. Damned hormones. "I was going to ask if you could set up a simple wireless system so we could share the internet connection."

"Of course I can set that up. I'll pick up a router at Fry's tomorrow."

"Thanks," Holly said to his back as he clomped downstairs, grateful that he was willing to do so much for her without question.

Nick knocked about downstairs for a while. Holly did her best to get comfortable and work through one of the many books friends had sent over, but wishing she had time to read more and actually having the time were two different things. Holly looked up when Nick came back into the room, grateful for the distraction.

"I have enough money, you know."

"Enough for what? I haven't asked you for anything." Except your heart, and I haven't gotten more than a fraction of that. She knew her thought was unfair. He did love her, in his own way, that was clear.

"I know that. It's just that you don't need to work. I make a pretty good living from my films, from Solstice. I can certainly support the both of us while you're on bed rest and after the baby is born."

Holly closed her eyes for a long moment, considering her response. "Thank you, Nick." It was the best Holly could come up with. It was sincerely a very nice gesture. It just wasn't what she was looking for from him. She wanted all of him, not his money.

They sat together for a moment in silence. "You're not going to take time off work, are you?" he said, matter-of-factly.

Holly shook her head. "No, Nick. I don't think I can afford to make that kind of sacrifice right now."

"Why? After seeing how much better you seem over the last few days, I think all of your focus should be on providing the best environment and rest for you and the baby."

Holly tried not to let her exasperation show. "That's all fine, but we don't have any kind of commitment beyond tomorrow, really. Do we?" When Nick didn't answer, Holly continued. "I'd love to not work while I'm on bed rest, Nick, but I don't want to spend my savings that way. Maybe I could catch up on all the projects I want to finish or try—like helping some of our organizations with grant proposals, or finally take up knitting little booties, I don't know. But, honestly, without any commitment, I don't feel like I could rely on your generosity that way. I don't really know what will ultimately happen with us or how we're going to raise our child, but I need to keep planning as if I'm going to raise him or her alone."

"You don't trust me."

"Of course I trust you, Nick. I love you. I would trust you with my life. That's not the issue here. The issue is that I don't know where we're going to be—and until you make a decision, I'm not going to change my plans."

Their routine changed after that. They both worked mornings, and spent the afternoons together instead. Getting to know him in this more intimate way was both wonderful and heartbreaking. On the one hand, it confirmed all the reasons she had fallen in love with him. He was kind, considerate, funny. On the other hand, the elephant in the living room—the issue of their commitment—didn't seem to be something he was thinking about. She was afraid of pushing him in case he said this was the end. She wasn't ready to end it—and she felt she was in no physical condition to add the stress of a breakup to her already fragile and tenuous hold on the pregnancy.

One night after dinner when they were in bed, Nick seemed more talkative than usual. He turned off the television that had been quietly playing in the background and propped himself up on the pillows, gazing at her.

"Tell me about your parents."

"There's not much to say," Holly said matter-of-factly. "They died when I was four, end of story." Holly did not like to talk about her parents. It brought up the feeling of being set adrift and the pain of longing to belong in a normal family.

"It sounds like the beginning of the story to me."

Holly sighed. "I don't remember much about my parents, to tell you the truth. They're more stiffly posing figures in old photographs than real people. They had me late in their marriage. They'd been together for twelve years, married ten, when I came into their lives. And even when I was a toddler, I don't think they really got used to having a child. After I was born, they continued their twice yearly, month-long vacations around the globe, always leaving me with Nana and Gramps from Thanksgiving until the New Year.

"Their last trip was to Greece in the late fall, around Thanksgiving. I remember because Nana and I were tracing our hands to make turkeys. They had rented a sailboat to tour the Greek islands, but the weather was rough going that November, and they capsized in an unexpected storm."

"You stayed with your grandparents after that?"

She nodded. "It was touch and go for a while, honestly. My grandparents weren't sure my parents were dead. I didn't understand for a long time what was going on, just that I wasn't ever going home again. After those first few days, or maybe weeks, I don't remember that well, they gave up hope. From what Gramps told me when I got older, eventually there were no more rescue efforts. And during the retrieval mission—that's what they call it when they think people are dead, but don't want to say it—my parents' remains were never found."

"Did you think they were still alive, that they would come back?"

Holly nodded, averting dampened eyes from Nick's. "Whenever I thought my grandparents were being too strict, I used to fantasize that my parents would come back and take me home. They never did."

"After growing up with my mom and dad, for all those years, I can't imagine a childhood without them."

She shook her head. "Don't feel sorry for me. I was blessed, Nick, because Nana and Gramps truly loved me, and I them. Sure, it was hard not having a young mom around who understood fashion, who was there when I got my first period or went to the prom. I mean, they were older and died while I was in college, so they weren't there when I met Drew. There was no one at my wedding to walk me down the aisle, that kind of thing.

"I certainly had all the material things. It wasn't the love I missed so much , because they truly cared for me and loved me deeply, you've got to understand that. It was just those critical life moments when I felt very lonely. I had to grow up quickly. I was on my own at an early age, and when they passed, I had no one to rely on but myself."

"Well, I'm here for you now," Nick said "We've got each other."

She stared at him, her mouth gaping. "How can you say that when you're still deciding on us, on whether or not we truly have a future? Don't you see how it seems like no matter what I do, someone is leaving me?"

"But I'm here, Holly. Be fair to me. I'm not Drew," Nick said.

"For how long?"

Nick sighed, clearly exasperated. "You're not being reasonable. I'm working through this, Holly. I'm trying here."

"Trying? There's a word a girl likes to hear," she said, her voice escalating. "I'm sorry that being with me is so difficult," she said quietly, her anger dying as quickly as it had flared up. She tried to swallow the tears that suddenly seemed to gather in her throat.

"It's not you, it's… "

Holly closed her eyes, caught in a memory, "Me. Yeah, I know, Drew, we've hashed it out all before."

Sixteen

The room was suddenly hushed as they both realized what she said.

"I'm so sorry," Holly said, immediately repentant. "I didn't mean that. I know you're not him."

Abruptly, Nick changed the subject, not looking her in the eye. "What are you hungry for tonight? I thought I'd pick up a salad for you from the Brazilian grill down the hill."

Holly was quiet for a long time, trying to decide what it would be best to say. "What are you going to have? I can't imagine a salad would be enough for you," Holly said very quietly, leaving the subject of their relationship on the back burner, letting him, and herself, off the hook for now. She looked at the clock Nick had added to the bedside table. "Besides, it's only two… "

"I'm going out for a few hours. I'll bring back dinner. I'll work it out, don't worry," Nick said with a tender smile. "I shouldn't be gone more than an hour. Do you want me to have Sophie come over to keep you company?"

"No, I'm fine," Holly said. Nick grabbed his keys, wallet, and jacket. She held her breath until she heard the front door close and his car engine start. Then the tears started coming and for several minutes would not stop. As she looked at her growing abdomen, she knew time was running out. What could be so awful about being with her and their baby that Nick couldn't pull the trigger and make a decision to stay?

She flipped open her cell and speed dialed Sophie.

The alarm in her friend's voice was immediate. "Are you okay? Is there anything wrong with the baby?"

"No, we're both fine. I just had the biggest fight with Nick," Holly said, sniffling.

"Need me to come over? I'm off strike duty for now." Sophie's union was on strike. She spent four hours every morning picketing at different studios.

"No, I'm all right." She paused, gathering her strength to tell her friend about the monumental blunder she made. "I called him Drew," Holly confessed, trying not to cringe at Sophie's sharp intake of breath. "I'm not even sure how it happened. We were talking about commitment and the baby, and it just slipped out. I didn't mean anything. I was just frustrated because I feel like I'm in the same boat I was in with Drew, only I'm not even married this time around."

Sophie was quiet for a long time. "But he's not Drew."

"My feelings are the same. I feel like I have some repellant that keeps men away."

"Holly, a baby, marriage, commitment, whatever are big steps for any guy. I know Nick pushed in the beginning. It's like he didn't know what to do with you once he caught you, but you've got to cut him a little slack. You may be ready to change your life, but maybe he isn't ready to change his."

"Then we should just go our separate ways, right? Staying here with him is only prolonging the inevitable, isn't it?" Sophie's response was non-committal, and Holly let her go when she realized there was the low rumble of a male voice in the background.

She felt trapped. She wished she could get up, go home this very moment, and nurse her hurt feelings, but the doctor's orders meant she had to stay put for now.

Nick slid into a booth at Norm's Diner on Pico Boulevard. His father was already there, large Coke in hand, straw in mouth, studying a menu he knew by heart. It had remained unchanged for as long as Nick could remember. The red vinyl booth dwarfed his father. Nick tried not to notice that the man he'd looked up to for years appeared smaller than he remembered. Nick pushed aside the plastic covered menu and leaned his elbows on the table. When the waitress came to take their order, they each got their "usual."

"So why did you bring me here?" Dominic asked. "I know it's not for the food. Not that I don't appreciate the grub, don't get me wrong."

"It's about Holly."

"I figured. Tell me something good."

"It is good, Dad, really good. I'm going to ask her to marry me." Nick sighed, and looked down at his entwined hands. "But I need everything to be just right before I propose to her."

Before he could continue, the waitress brought their food. Dominic immediately poured steak sauce on his meat and ketchup on his potatoes. Nick looked at the plate drowned in sauce, and thought the eggs were lucky enough to get away scot free, until his father picked up the picante sauce and started twisting off the cap. Shaking his head, Nick dug into his unadorned Lumberjack breakfast, which amounted to a lot of everything from the breakfast menu on one plate, even though it was three in the afternoon.

"What's this about everything being right? You should just ask her already. The girl—excuse me, woman—has waited long enough."

"Dad, it's because she has waited this long that I want to do it right."

"I don't agree with your sense of timing—it's all screwed up if you ask me—but I'll help you with whatever you need," he said, waving away Nick's protest.

The two men leaned across the table, their heads almost touching as they pushed aside their half-eaten meals and made their plans.

Dominic poked his head around the doorjamb and tipped his paint-splattered cap to Holly during the beginning of her third week of confinement. "I'll try to be as quiet as possible," he said, by way of greeting. "Nick and I are just finishing up some things on the house."

"No need to be quiet on my account. I am not sick. I keep telling Nick that, but he's been treating me like an invalid," she said, shaking her head. "Anyway, do what you guys have to do.

Impasse

I know getting work done on this house is important to him," Holly said graciously. "I'm keeping busy myself."

For a couple of days, Nick didn't do any work in the loft. There was a lot of stuff going on around the house, hammering, banging, painting, and a little cursing. Holly admired the way Nick and his dad could work together, sometimes arguing but mostly laughing. She couldn't wait until she was well enough to see what they'd done with the rest of the house. She knew Dominic would make her child a wonderful grandfather.

On the one-month anniversary of her emergency room visit, Holly had an appointment with the obstetrician. Nick had offered to go, but she rebuffed him and asked Sophie to go along instead. Since her best friend had volunteered to be her birth coach, she wanted to keep things consistent. It was too up in the air with Nick for her to begin relying on him.

After the checkup, Sophie drove Holly back to Nick's house.

"What are you going to do? Go home?" That was the question of the hour. Dr. Cole had modified his previous order. Holly was thrilled that she was no longer on strict bed rest. She was still pretty much confined to the house, but she could get up and walk around a little more, as long as she agreed to spend most of the day off her feet.

"I don't know. I'm just happy that Dr. Cole modified the order. The bedroom is fine, but I was feeling a little claustrophobic."

Nick came to the front door as soon as their car pulled up. He was poised to help Holly out of the car when she surprised him by opening the car door herself and stepping out.

"What are you doing? Do you want me to help you upstairs?" Nick asked, looking concerned.

Holly's face lit up in a smile. "I won't need you to help me around anymore," she said doing a small pirouette. "Dr. Cole lightened my sentence. I'm only on 'house arrest' right now. I can walk around some."

Despite her words, Nick scooped her in his arms and carried her upstairs, placing her gently in a dining room chair. Sophie followed, carrying Holly's bag. Her friend put the bags on the table and made herself comfortable, while Nick puttered around the kitchen making tea and sandwiches for them.

When Nick brought the food to the table, Holly and Sophie added cream and sugar to their tea. He tore into the sandwiches, and they ate and drank in silence for a few minutes. Holly put down her tea, and leveled her gaze at Nick. She had decided once and for all. "I'm going home, Nick."

He met her gaze with his own. "What exactly did the doctor say?"

"Dr. Cole said that I was doing much better, and I could walk around a bit as long as I stayed pretty much in the house and sat for most of the day."

"I think we need to talk about this before you take such a drastic action."

"It's not 'drastic,' Nick. I'm just doing what I should have done four weeks ago. We've said all that needs to be said." The trill of Sophie's cell phone ring tone broke the tension in the room. Sophie answered the call and cupped her hand around the handset while walking over to the cold fireplace, well out of earshot.

"Before you go, there's something I need to show you," Nick said, his voice rough with emotion. He gently grasped her hand

Impasse

on the table, caressing it with his own.

Sophie came back to the table, sensing the tension between them. She waved the phone dramatically, "Um, that's my cue." She leaned down to grab her bag and bussed Holly on the cheek. "I'll give you a call later," she said and bounced out of the room.

Holly swept her gaze back to Nick's. "What do you want to show me?"

He gently guided her upstairs. At the top, Nick opened the door to the second bedroom. Holly gasped, unprepared for the sight before her. Nick had created a nursery more beautiful than her wildest dreams. The walls were a warm yellow, the color of sweet potato flesh.

Her grandmother's antique mahogany rocker sat near the French doors, which opened onto a small deck that he'd cleaned and painted. An antique nursery dresser, topped with a changing table, was opposite the rocking chair. Nick had also purchased a new crib.

Holly sat heavily in the chair, feeling like her legs could no longer hold her.

Nick knelt beside her, first smoothing her hair, then holding her hands in his. "Where did you get the crib?" Holly asked, not able to think of anything else to say.

"I know this isn't from your family. When I was reading about cribs on the internet, though, I realized that new cribs were much safer for babies. This one best matched the furniture you already had. It's one way we could start a new tradition.

"I know the room is not finished," Nick rambled on, clearly anxious about her reaction to all this, "but I couldn't figure out what kind of curtains or blinds or drapes you might want. I made measurements, and I thought maybe you could pick something out at an online store, or if you know of something at a local store, I'll order it or pick it up for you."

She shook her head again, trying to figure out what he was trying to say. "Are you asking me to stay?"

He nodded. "I love you, Holly. You're the most beautiful, most amazing woman I've ever known. I love your hair," he said reaching up to stroke her curls. "I love your body. You overwhelm me. I can't imagine ever not wanting you. I know that I've made this hard for both of us, but I want to do this right once and for all." Nick stood slowly and removed a small velvet box from the top drawer of the dresser. He knelt again, this time on one knee. "I love you, Holly, and I love our child whoever he or she turns out to be. Will you marry me?"

"Are you certain about this?" Holly asked, suddenly feeling very unsure. It felt like every nerve in her body was on alert, quivering in anticipation of her response. "You don't have a couch," she blurted out.

He didn't even blink at her non sequitur. "I know how much you love your grandparents' things. I didn't get anything for the living room because I hoped you would bring your settee here to make it your home as much as mine."

Holly was at a loss for words then. "Oh," was all she managed to say.

He nodded solemnly. "I know I've taken a long time to come to this. But I'm surer of this than I've ever been of anything."

It was overwhelming to know that everything she'd ever wanted was within her grasp, a man she loved deeply, a baby to complete their family. Finally, a sense of belonging. She looked at the emerald solitaire that was more perfect for her than any diamond she'd ever seen, and nodded yes. Her throat was too constricted with emotion to say the words.

He slid the ring on her finger and kissed her soundly, deeply. It was a kiss of promise, of hope, of the future, of always.

Epilogue

Early morning light cast a bluish glow on Holly's face as she rocked the sleepy baby in her arms. The infant had just nursed and should sleep for a few hours at least, giving Holly time to rest. She was ready to lay her child in the mahogany crib when Iris's bright green eyes popped open, roaming the room. Holly scooped the baby in her arms again and turned to face the door where her fiancé Nick leaned against the frame. Her fiancé. The words rang in her mind like a dream come true. After all their setbacks, it still amazed her that this wonderful man had come into her life. He was gorgeous, charming, loving, and all hers. Letting his age blind her to his love had been her biggest mistake. She was glad they had made their peace with it before their fears had crushed their love.

"Is she asleep?" Nick whispered.

"No, she was about to drift off but opened her eyes when her daddy walked into the room."

Impasse

Nick took the drowsy baby from Holly's arms and cradled her against his shoulder. Like magic, the baby dropped off.

Holly shook her head wonderingly. "It happens every time."

Holly dropped back into the leather-padded rocking chair, bone weary. Nick kneeled next to her, swallowing her hands in his.

"I never thanked you."

"For what?" Holly asked.

"For honoring my mother like you did. I was truly moved when you announced to everyone in the delivery room that our daughter would be called Iris."

"She sounds like she was a wonderful woman. I know that she surely raised an amazing son. I wish I'd had the chance to get to know her," Holly said wistfully.

"Mom would have loved you as much as I do."

"I hope our daughter can live up to the name," Holly said.

"I'm sure she will," Nick said. They both rose quietly, being sure not to disturb the baby, and walked to the bedroom, whispering about the upcoming wedding and planning their future.

About the Author

Sylvie Fox is the author of smart women's fiction. Her compelling stories are boldly told, designed to keep readers turning the pages. Whether you're reading Sylvie's romantic women's fiction or legal thrillers, she wants you to enjoy the heroine's journey.

She splits her time between Los Angeles and Budapest, where she enjoys yoga, knitting, farm-to-table cooking, and life with her husband and son. When she's not writing, her nose is stuck in a book.

Made in the USA
Columbia, SC
22 September 2020